REVIVED HOPE

PREQUEL TO THE BAY TOWN SERIES

KATHLEEN J. ROBISON

ISBN: 978-1-951839-37-6

Celebrate Lit Publishing

304 S. Jones Blvd #754

Las Vegas, NV, 89107

http://www.celebratelitpublishing.com/

Therefore we also, since we are surrounded by so great a cloud of witnesses, let us lay aside every weight, and the sin which so easily ensnares *us,* and let us run with endurance the race that is set before us, looking unto Jesus, the [a]author and [b]finisher of *our* faith, who for the joy that was set before Him endured the cross, despising the shame, and has sat down at the right hand of the throne of God.

Hebrews 12:1-2

To my parents, Milton Jaquish Bacon and Shizuko Tome Higa Bacon.
Thank you for being who you were and trusting your lives to Jesus.

CHAPTER 1

The old, one-story, red-brick structure stood proud and protective, yet Melanie hesitated as she positioned herself across the street, her stomach churning. She smoothed down her pencil skirt and tugged at the matching off-white blazer. The snug suit fitted her trim figure well, and the feel of the linen fabric boosted her confidence. *Power suit,* she thought, but a nagging doubt crept into her mind.

The afternoon sun heated her body, and Melanie was thankful for the cool breeze. She wondered if only in California could there be a heatwave this early in the year. She glanced upward, thinking of her future. Being in control of your ambitions was the easy philosophy of the times. Surrendering them to God was difficult, and that's what she had been trying to do when her dreams fell into her lap. It wasn't exactly the way Melanie had envisioned, but when opportunity knocked, she couldn't say no. *Could she?* Now she wasn't so sure. *Stay calm,* she told herself. *A strong, confident thirty-two-year-old woman has got this.*

She waited for the flashing hand to signal the countdown, beckoning her to cross the street. Melanie glanced back at the parking lot behind her. Her brand new, sporty Ford Mustang glistened, an impulse extravagance in celebration of the news of inheriting the bridal shop.

"Walk now," came the staccato voice from the crosswalk box.

Melanie took a step off the curb, and her ankle wobbled.

HONK! A sharp, threatening sound blared.

She stumbled back onto the sidewalk as a silver vehicle made a sharp right-hand turn, almost brushing her body. She grabbed the light post, and the car disappeared before she could identify anything other than the color.

"Idiot!" She yelled, then looked down—*stupid shoes,* she thought.

She wished she would have worn the pumps. As her racing heart settled, a nervous chuckle escaped. She loved trendy footwear, although she often regretted it. Still, it never seemed to impede her work performance. Everyone, including her father, told her she was good at what she did. Great, in fact. Her organizational skills were perfect for her home-based business, wedding consulting.

Melanie's services brought in the extra income she needed to support herself and her teenage daughter. She was on the verge of doing it full-time as soon as she could move from home to an actual office. Whenever she met a client, it had to be at a coffee shop or a restaurant. Her yearning for office space and the dream of owning a storefront shop had finally come true. Yet, before she could admire the new address on her business card, reality threatened to become a dream once more.

The light changed, and Melanie strode through the crosswalk, straight to the old door that read "Law Offices of William L. Randall." She pushed it open, and the secretary greeted Melanie, pointing to the door behind. Pulling back her shoulders, Melanie straightened as she brushed back a few escaped brown strands from the loose bun piled atop her head.

"Good morning, Mr. Randall."

"Mrs. Thompson, please have a seat. This won't take long." He shuffled some papers, and though he smiled, his bushy gray brows hung ominously above his eyes. "I looked over the lease agreement to the shop, and the owner may have grounds to evict you."

"But Nina had a two-year lease."

Nina was the former owner who died and willed the shop to Melanie. She wasn't a relative, but Nina had no children, and Melanie was a faithful, long-time shop employee.

Fifteen years ago, as a single teen, she had a baby to support, and Melanie's mother was a seamstress at the shop and introduced them. Nina gave her a chance, and Melanie worked hard, proving herself worthy. Although Melanie never intended to own a retail bridal gown business, her home-based wedding planning services were a good fit.

"Yes, she did. Unfortunately, the lease was in her name only."

The validity of the lease had never entered Melanie's mind. As the buyer and advertising rep, she helped to grow Nina's business. She knew some finance and business aspects, but not enough. Her knowledge came from working closely with Nina, but most were on the marketing side, not the retail business.

She looked up at Mr. Randall. "Okay, now what?"

"First off, this eviction notice isn't an eviction order. It's like a letter of intent. Did you respond yet?"

"No, I wanted to hear what you had to say first."

"Well, I'm not a real estate attorney, but you might consider hiring one."

Melanie had slaved all these years, putting away practically every penny for her own office while working for Nina. She envisioned her nest egg floating upwards in dollar signs.

"All right. How much will that cost?"

Mr. Randall spread his hands on the desk in front of him.

"That all depends. Initial costs roughly one-thousand dollars, then they'll bill hourly, perhaps four-hundred an hour."

Melanie's mouth gaped.

"For a good attorney, that is," said Mr. Randall.

"I don't have that kind of money. We'll just move." Melanie tended to speak rashly when her confidence waned. "How hard can that be?"

She knew if she moved, her clientele would follow. The brides loved her, and her helpful manner was the catalyst for launching her services. The brides asked for her suggestions and help, and it had finally allowed her to start her own at-home business.

"Mrs. Thompson, moving can be costly, as well." He nodded. "That figure I quoted is if you require legal counsel. You may not. Would you like me to respond to the notice? Then we can go from there."

"Could you do that?"

"Of course. Let's take care of this right now." He picked up the phone and dialed.

As Melanie listened, his end of the conversation didn't sound like it was going well. In fact, when Mr. Randall hung up, he took a deep breath and shook his head. His lips drew into a tight line. "I'll ask my secretary to get some referrals of real estate attorneys for you. The owner appears to be difficult. I'm sorry, Mrs. Thompson."

Heat waves filtered from the sidewalk, and Melanie unbuttoned her blazer. She pulled at her loose, silky cami-top and breathed deeply, sputtering her lips in exasperation. Replacing her sunglasses, she stared up at the scorching sun. Somehow, God would work this out. She just had to trust.

Melanie pulled out her phone to call her father. As a single mom of a teenager, she sought his counsel first. Her father was always there for her-- the first person she turned to when in trouble. That hadn't always been the case.

Before calling, she heard footsteps, and a shadow cooled her back from the sun. She turned.

A tall, large man stood behind her. A burgundy dress shirt spread tightly across his broad shoulders, and a plain black tie hung down his muscled chest. Gold framed sunglasses perched atop his shiny, shaved white head. After staring at her, he lowered the glasses, covering his small, beady eyes. He pulled a cigarette from a pack in his front pocket and pulled out a lighter. The demonstrative clicks of the cap made her flinch. A flame flared, and the lighter flipped shut. Smoking was illegal in public. That was the first thing that crossed her mind. *How bold of him.*

Melanie looked away. When the light turned, he stepped off the curb, and she remained. He never looked back, and she waited for the next light and kept her distance, just the same. As she watched, he slipped into a silver sedan parked across the street.

When she finally reached her car, she whooshed out a forceful breath and kicked her front tire. As if this was all the fault of her brand-new Ford Mustang. Melanie thought about the shop as she drove. It fared well and fed a steady line of brides her way. Maybe she could afford to move rather than fight the landlord.

She clocked in for the day but then stopped and chuckled. As the owner, it wasn't necessary anymore. She did the purchasing and marketing in the shop, but all the wedding planning she did at home, after hours.

Walking into the building, she smiled at Gloria, the assistant manager who had pretty much run the place since Nina's death. She hadn't worked for Nina as long as Melanie, but they quickly became fast friends. A few sales associates and a part-time accountant were the only other employees.

"Hi, Melanie. How'd it go?" Gloria glanced up from her desk.

"The landlord intends to evict us."

"That's what I was afraid of. The building owner is not a nice guy. He's been trying to get Nina out ever since he bought the building."

"How come I never knew that?" Melanie's brow furrowed.

"Nina kept it from everyone but me. I was here when she got a harassing phone call and another time when he threatened to sue her. It was usually after everyone had gone home."

"I'm really surprised she said nothing to me."

"She didn't want you to worry. You were her baby." Gloria shrugged. "You were like the daughter she never had. Parents protect their kids, right?"

Melanie knew that feeling. She smiled, thinking of her own teenage daughter, Lacey. Heaven forbid anyone who tried to hurt her. "Yes, you're right."

"Besides, Nina didn't want the employees or customers thinking she might close up or move or something worse. What did Mr. Randall say?"

"He said the new landlord may have grounds to evict because I'm not on the lease. Was it him that harassed Nina?"

"Probably, and there was this scary-looking guy that came in late once, just before closing. I mean, what guy walks in to look at wedding gowns all by himself? It gave me the creeps." Gloria shivered.

Melanie recalled the man on the street at the crosswalk. He appeared suddenly, she thought, and right outside the law office. "What did he look like?" she asked.

CHAPTER 2

A bell jingled in the distance, interrupting their conversation. Squeals pierced the air, and applause erupted. Melanie and Gloria joined in the excitement of a bride finding her perfect gown. It was a celebration ritual for the bride to ring a bell when she settled on "the dress." For Melanie, it was always bittersweet.

Seeing the bride and her entourage enjoying the merriment distracted Melanie. As if in a dream, she stepped forward, floating alongside a rack of gowns. She brushed a hand past the thick plastic coverings over each white dress. The sparkling sequins and seed pearls never ceased to lift her spirits. Yards of lace, tulle, and satin brushed against her legs as she walked down the line. Weddings and wedding dresses. Something she'd never personally experienced. Every young woman's dream, but a lost one for her.

"So, Gloria, the strange-looking guy?"

"Oh, yes. He came once but made a weird comment, like, 'You got some beautiful dresses here.' Asked about our inventory and said something like, 'What a shame it would be to lose it all.'"

"Why, that's a threat, isn't it? Did you report him?"

"No, and he stopped in another time too, but Tito kicked him out. You know Tito. He's got a short fuse."

Chuckling, Melanie pictured the aggressive short, stout Tito. She was grateful for the accountant, who did an excellent job of keeping the books. He also kept Melanie well informed of what was happening with the finances.

Ding-a-ling-a-ling! Ding-a-ling!

Everyone cheered and clapped again. Melanie turned to see another youthful woman with long blond hair down to her waist spinning around. She wore a Renaissance-style gown, and a wreath-like crown of white flowers and greenery crowned her head. Every bit a Guinevere waiting for her Sir Lancelot. It reminded her of old medieval movies.

"Business is good, huh?" Melanie turned to Gloria.

"Well, the dresses are selling, but business costs are going up. California is no friend to small enterprise."

"What do you mean?"

"The employee thing. You know, taxes, pensions, medical benefits."

"I see." She'd never thought about that. Being an "employer" with her home-based business was another small business entity she hadn't intended to experience.

Melanie's father knew all that stuff. He was excited for her, but it had always been his dream to be an entrepreneur. Still, Melanie had caught his vision. When Melanie started her home-based business, he was enthusiastic and proud of her, but now, the shop was an added plus. She almost couldn't believe she was here after her rocky start.

A twinge grabbed her heart. It always did when she recalled her poor adolescent choices of fifteen years ago. She'd crushed her dad and mom back then. Although thoughts of her pregnancy before marriage still plagued her, warmth enveloped her whenever she thought about the direction her life took now. What a difference. Her father had been so angry and devastated when she broke the news that she was pregnant, but he was now her biggest supporter through the changes that faith had made in their lives. He'd been the one who pushed her to branch out with her wedding services. She was a natural, and the years she spent coordinating weddings at their church gave her lots of experience. And now this. It was more than she ever imagined. God's promises. That's what her father always said nowadays.

Melanie shook herself and looked at Gloria, hunched over the desk. She was a hard worker, too. Really, the brains behind the business. Melanie had so much to learn from her.

"Gloria, I don't know why you're the assistant manager. You're more knowledgeable about running a retail business than I am. How about you take the title of manager, not an assistant?"

"You know plenty about the business, Melanie."

"Well, buying and some marketing, but you handle everything else." Melanie glanced at the two sales associates. "And the girls love you. You treat them well."

"Well, I guess it wouldn't be much different from now, right?"

"Right. You keep doing what you're doing, and I'll keep doing what I'm doing."

"Great! Do I get a raise?"

"If we can afford it, absolutely. We have a tight budget, but I'll check with Tito."

"Well, I can forget the raise then. Tito's always complaining about how close we are to going in the red."

"It's not that bad. That's just Tito. He's cautious. We went over the books recently. We can make some cuts to make it happen." Melanie hugged her, but the turmoil inside conflicted with what the future held. As she turned, a sharply dressed man stepped through the entrance.

She glanced past him, and her eye caught a flash of burgundy on a tall man remaining outside. He lowered his gold-framed sunglasses, causing Melanie's eyes to widen. *Was it the guy at the crosswalk?* She couldn't be sure. The man in the suit approached her.

"Hello, I'm looking for the shop owner."

Gloria stared. "Who are you?"

"I'm the legal counsel for the owner of this building."

Melanie suppressed a chuckle. *Figures. He looks like the young Michael Corleone from the old Godfather movie.*

"Oh, you mean the new guy who is trying to kick us out. We have a two-year lease, you know. Still another year to go." Gloria stood with her hands on her hips.

"Are you Melanie Thompson?" He looked directly at Melanie and not Gloria.

"I am."

"May I speak with you in private?"

They retreated to Nina's old office, and Melanie asked Gloria to join them. *Michael Corleone* wasted no time.

"The two-year lease the previous owner signed is no longer valid, seeing as your name is not on it."

"I'm sure there's some condition in there. Isn't there?" Melanie said sweetly.

"I'm sorry, I'm not at liberty to give you legal counsel." He smirked.

Gloria narrowed her eyes. "You want us out."

"Yes. She's right." He nodded at Gloria. "The owner wants you to vacate the premises, and my client would like to take possession as soon as possible."

"My attorney just responded to your letter today. How much time do we have?"

He pulled a letter from his pocket. "Thirty days. Here's your eviction notice."

Gloria laughed. "You're kidding, right? Or what? What if we're not out in a month?"

Melanie halted Gloria with a raised hand and spoke to the lawyer. "Thank you. My attorney will contact you."

He stood. "The most he can buy you is about three months. I suggest you make plans now."

"I thought you couldn't give legal counsel?" Gloria spat out the words.

"I'm merely suggesting that it would be a good idea."

He was gone before Melanie could ask him to leave. A quick call to Mr. Randall assured her that he could file a postponement of the eviction, but they would need to meet soon. The women returned to their work, but Melanie closed her office door and sat. Bowing her head, she prayed for guidance in her new unknown future.

CHAPTER 3

At the week's end, Melanie was grateful that it was finally Friday as she drove to her parents' house to pick up her daughter. They helped her out by picking up Lacey after school most afternoons, and Melanie picked her up at their home after work.

"How was school?"

"Good," said Lacey while eating ice cream and playing Yahtzee with Rick, Melanie's father.

She admired her father and all he'd done for her, but a twinge of pain hit her heart. That guilt again. Long ago, when Melanie was not much older than Lacey was now, she began lying and sneaking out—going to parties with friends. It ended in her getting pregnant and running away with her baby's father shortly after high school graduation.

Lacey mumbled as she licked each spoonful of rich chocolate ice cream. "This is the best chocolate peanut butter I ever had!"

"It's a chocolate caramel swirl," said Rick.

"Whatever. Can I have seconds?" Lacey grinned.

"No. We haven't had dinner yet. And why are you eating ice cream now?"

"Hey, Lacey! Come, finish the rest of this ice cream, so

your grandfather doesn't eat it all later. It's not good for his health," Patricia, Melanie's mother, called from the kitchen.

"Well, Grandma's the man. Gotta listen to her!" Lacey grabbed her bowl, bounding from the table.

Rick chuckled and eyed Melanie. "How did the meeting with the attorney go?"

"He thinks I should get a real estate lawyer. The landlord is evicting me."

"You got a notice?"

"Today." She slumped down. "I don't know if I have it in me to fight this." She'd been mulling over it all week, and her dream was becoming a nightmare.

"You do."

"No. I'm not a fighter. That's Charlene." Her sister, seven years her senior, was a strong, independent woman. Melanie tried to think of herself the same way. She didn't always believe it.

"You can say that again. But so are you. When you want something, you go after it. Honey, hang on to what you've got. The shop isn't going anywhere. It's yours for now."

Melanie had never dreamed of owning a retail business. She only longed to have an office, a little wedding shop to meet and service her clients. She wondered if inheriting the shop was worth the trouble or expense. It might also detract from her business of helping brides make their dreams come true.

"I don't mean to sound ungrateful, and Nina's shop seemed like a Godsend, but I'm not so sure anymore." She drummed her fingers. "Dad, I think I might pursue that small business loan at the bank, just in case. I'll need it to retain an attorney, and if I get evicted, well…."

Her father was not a fan of credit. Rick stared at Melanie, his lips white. "Why don't you hold off? A lot has happened in the last month. You need time to pray about this. Besides, there is another option."

"Come on, Dad. I'm not asking anyone for money. A small business loan would mean I wouldn't have to do that. I don't want you and Mom to help. You've done so much for me already."

"I didn't offer." Rick winked.

"Well, I didn't expect you to, and I don't want to ask Charlene. She's up to her neck fighting justice in D.C."

Charlene lived frugally, but the death of her husband had left her more than comfortable financially, and she was extremely generous in offering help to Melanie.

"I guess I could ask Chris."

Another touchy subject. Her ex-husband was a thorn in everyone's side. Rick straightened his broad shoulders and shook his head. "No. Don't bring him into this."

"I know, Dad. Chris isn't very dependable."

"No, he never has been. Maybe never will be. And you'll regret it."

A hint of control marred his voice, and his eyes hardened. Melanie shivered, remembering her father before he came to a believing faith that had transformed his life. Rick had long ago expressed his forgiveness for Chris's abandonment of their daughter and granddaughter, but he struggled with a deadbeat dad popping in and out of their lives. In the eyes of a father, it was inexcusable. But his faith taught him otherwise, and Melanie hated that it caused him and her mother so much pain.

His eyes brightened. "Actually, I was thinking of the Restoration Grant. We just need to complete the application."

Rick, always the adventurer, had searched grants for start-up businesses. There weren't many in California, but he found one in the deep south.

"I can't believe you'd want me to move to Mississippi. We've talked about this. I don't think it's an option."

After the big hurricane, a small town issued grants for business owners to start or move their business there. Rick got excited at the prospect, solely because they'd lived in that town when Melanie and her sister were young.

"You never know." His brows rose. "It could be a fresh start."

"A fresh start from what? You already gave me that, Dad. You and Mom. Besides, Mississippi is a long way away."

Her cell rang, and though it was a welcome distraction from their conversation, respect for her father caused her to ignore it.

"Go ahead, Mel." Rick smiled.

She looked at the screen and frowned. "Oh. Hi, Chris." Noting the shake of her father's head, she stepped onto the back patio.

"Saturday? I'll have to check with Lacey... I have an appointment on Saturday... Beverly Hills? My appointment is at 11:30 in Culver City, near there... Okay, if Lacey wants to go, I'll drop her off. Just text me the info... and I'll get back with...." He clicked off before Melanie finished. She dropped her arm and huffed.

She stepped inside, and her mother glanced at her from the kitchen. Chris's phone call made everyone uncomfortable. Everyone but Lacey.

"Was that Chris?" Lacey asked rather casually. She always referred to him as Chris instead of Dad.

"Yes, it was your father. He wants to take you to lunch on Saturday."

"Again?"

"Yes, in Beverly Hills."

"Oooh, fancy!" Lacey squealed.

Patricia chuckled. "Figures. That's Chris. Footloose and fancy-free. Hasn't changed a bit." She glanced at Lacey. "I'm being judgy. I'm sorry, Lacey. Your dad is a lot of fun. I'll give him that."

But Chris had never been around much. After Melanie got pregnant, they had a hasty Las Vegas wedding. As her pregnancy progressed, Melanie couldn't keep up the partying that permeated their lives, and Chris soon found her a drag. The marriage lasted all but a few months. Hurt, humiliated, and haunted by what her future held, she had nowhere to turn. But Charlene stepped in. With her sister's help, she found the strength to cut Chris loose and struggled on without him. At Lacey's birth, she was reunited with her parents, but it wasn't till Lacey was five that Chris got back in touch. He came around once a year for her birthday.

"No worries. I know Chris is kind of flakey." Lacey shrugged. "Hey, Grandpa, how about another quick game of Yahtzee?"

"Sure, come on." Rick led the way to the living room.

Melanie joined her mother at the kitchen sink, grabbing a dishrag to wipe. "Sorry about that, Mom."

"Chris is her father. No two ways around that."

"How did you handle it, Mom? I mean, Charlene's dad?"

Patricia stared out the kitchen window. "Her father was never her dad." She leaned into Melanie. "My circumstances were much different than yours."

They rarely discussed Patricia's out-of-wedlock pregnancy, but Melanie's mom held nothing back when asked. Patricia had gotten pregnant in high school, and the boy was much like Chris, only younger. A teenager like her.

And then there was Rick, the older, stable neighbor friend. He and Patricia's older brother had been buddies forever, and Patricia often hung with them growing up. Over time, Rick's feelings for the kid sister changed. He admired Patricia from a distance, and when she was left abandoned, Rick was there for her. Home from a job abroad, he stuck around, helping her through the abandonment and emotional rollercoaster.

"Like they say, the rest is history. I fell in love with your dad, and we married before Charlene was even born." Patricia smiled at her daughter.

Melanie had heard the story before. It made her admire her dad even more. "What about Charlene's dad?"

"After high school graduation, he enlisted in the military, and I never saw him again," said Patricia.

"That's right. I remember now. I'm not sure I could handle Chris never coming around." She blinked tightly, wishing she hadn't expressed that. "I mean, not that I want him to, but for Lacey's sake."

"I had Rick. Your father became Charlene's dad, and neither of us ever doubted his love. However, he struggled with raising two daughters in this world, and he worried that some boy would take advantage of you two, and the cycle would repeat itself."

Melanie's stomach knotted, and she whispered, "Mom? Dad didn't blame you for my pregnancy, did he?"

"Not at all, sweetheart. He blamed nothing on me, but still, he struggled. Your dad never wanted you or your sister to experience the rejection I did before he stepped in."

"That's why Dad was so over-protective." Melanie sighed. "And I messed up anyway."

"Well, we all blunder, don't we? Maybe your father and I were wound a little too tight. Hanging on to the outside, but not working on the inside." She pointed to Melanie's heart. "Neither of us knew the Lord back then, but the things we've learned and the mistakes we've made just give us that much more grace for others."

Patricia dried her hands and hugged her daughter. "You'll navigate life with or without Chris. Just include God in everything." She frowned. "No, don't include Him. Put God first."

"Thanks, Mom."

"Now, don't forget. I pray for you two every day. I even pray for Chris, sometimes."

"Okay." Melanie kissed her mom's cheek. "Well, we better run." Melanie turned. "Lacey, let's go."

"Already? I only beat her twice." Rick teased.

"Well, you've been playing this game before I was even born!" Lacey poked her grandfather.

As they walked out the door, Rick tapped Melanie's shoulder. "The grant?"

"I'll pray about it, Daddy. Love you guys."

CHAPTER 4

S aturday morning, standing in front of her closet, Melanie grabbed another dress.

"Arrgh!" She groaned, disliking that she was a tad annoyed at how excited Lacey was to see her dad. Who was she fooling? Melanie took too much care getting dressed herself and hated to admit that Chris still stirred a little something within her. His rejection had left deep scars, but his charm still had a hold on her.

Saturday traffic was better than a weekday, but Southern California rush hour was basically all day, every day. The cars moved at a slow pace, both north and south on the 405 freeway.

"Lacey, here's the deal. I'll drop you off for lunch with your dad, and I'm heading over to my florist." Melanie glanced over her shoulder, switching lanes.

"Mom, don't you think this seems weird. He already took me out on my birthday and another time this year for no reason. What's up with that?"

The old pain rose, and Melanie gulped, trying to stuff it down. It wasn't that she wanted him back. It's just that thinking about what could have been occasionally muddled her brain. "Well, maybe he's getting soft in his old age. I mean, you are fifteen now. He doesn't have to deal with temper tantrums."

"He's never been around long enough for that, Mom. How about I turn on the hormone thing? That will really mess him up." Lacey grabbed her stomach and doubled over as if in pain.

A chuckle escaped, and Melanie stopped. "Lacey, that's not funny." Melanie made a concentrated effort to sound firm, but they both giggled.

Lacey plugged her iPhone into the radio speakers. Melanie's soft opera on the radio was silenced by the pounding beat of Lacey's rap music. The beautiful arias always inspired Melanie when planning a wedding, and she had a spectacular one coming up.

The bride and groom were from generations of high society, long-established in Los Angeles. If all went well, referrals from the bride and the vendors she was hiring would boost her recognition. It was the most high-end event she'd ever planned. Thinking about it caused her to glance outward for a moment. The clear blue skies reminded her to give thanks.

Melanie maneuvered the construction chaos when she pulled off the freeway. The abandoned buildings and graffiti faded away as they approached palm tree-lined streets and well-manicured lawns. Following her maps app, she turned at a diagonal intersection.

Lacey whistled at the massive gold, glass, and granite buildings. "Whoa! Look at this. Where are the celebrities?"

Shops and establishments rose all around them. Rodeo Drive was most definitely close by. When Melanie found the ritzy café Chris had chosen, it looked like it could be in Paris. Market umbrellas shaded the petite, round, linen-covered tables that dotted the sidewalks. A single white rosebud sat atop each table, and wooden bistro chairs surrounded each one. Melanie pulled her car into the parking lot, waving off the young valet.

"Just dropping off," said Melanie.

Chris's bushy blonde hair waved in the breeze. A classic V-neck tee shirt and expensive blue jeans framed his fit build. He flailed his arms and appeared to be arguing with a large man in a dark suit. The man was leaning against a sleek, black SUV with tinted windows. His jacket stretched taut over his crossed arms.

"Forget it. I told you, I'm finished with you guys. Get someone else." Chris yelled as he ran a hand through his thick hair. "I got to go. I'm meeting my wife and daughter for lunch."

Melanie stared. *Ex-wife, Chris. It's ex.*

Chris looked over and waved. A broad grin spread across his face, and he sauntered to Melanie's car. "Hey, Mel. Hi, Lacey."

He was so easygoing, even in chaos. "Trouble, Chris?" Melanie raised a brow. "Are you sure this is a good day for Lacey?"

"Yes. Of course, it is. Pshhh! No worries."

He opened the passenger door for Lacey, but she leaned over before exiting, giving Melanie a hug. Lacey jumped out, and Chris squeezed her with one arm. As he slammed the passenger door, Melanie jumped, but he smiled that flashy, charming smile. She tried not to notice.

"So, Mel, not going to join us?"

"Maybe another time. Lacey, I'll be back in about an hour." With her foot still on the brake, she put the car in drive. "Make healthy choices!"

As Melanie drove away, she overheard Chris say, "She still doing that?"

It reminded her how annoying he could be, and she tucked the ammunition away—a guard on her heart.

Driving to her favorite florist, Melanie thought how she

appreciated the relationships she'd built with vendors in Southern California. She was making a name for herself, and she wanted her father to be proud. The thought often permeated her actions.

Pulling up to the store, Melanie parked and stepped out. She smiled at the window decorated with twigs, ribbons, and twinkling lights. The wide-open double French doors of the family-run business welcomed her. Removing her sunglasses, she smiled as she entered. Flowers always took her breath away—refreshing, inspiring, and somehow humbling.

Exotic, slender-finger-like flowers drew her eye. Gently tugging out a stem, she breathed deep but coughed... repeatedly.

The shopkeeper laughed as she greeted Melanie and pointed to the tall, galvanized bucket of yellow flowers. "Yling-Ylang."

Melanie choked and sputtered. "These are bright and strong!"

"Yes, and a story behind them. A little-known flower in America, back in 1921, Coco Chanel discovered it as a secret ingredient in her famous perfume, and now they're popular again."

"Wow! I didn't know that. I'm impressed."

The older woman with disheveled hair wearing an old lab coat stained with green and brown plant smudges shrugged and grinned sheepishly.

"Well, they are beautiful, but this bride is going more for the earthy look." Melanie replaced the stem. "I'm thinking succulents, eucalyptus leaves. The trendy thing, right? On the other hand, it has to be dazzling, and those just might stand out enough." Melanie winked. "No one knows flowers better than you."

The woman flushed. "An excellent choice, but perhaps just a few."

Melanie finished up and waved goodbye. It was too early

to meet up with Lacey, so she sat in her car and took out her phone. She answered emails, made a few social media posts, and checked off some tasks. Turning her wrist, she looked at her watch. Still early. She tapped her steering wheel and finally started the engine. *Well, I guess I can try to be civil towards Chris.* She drove to the café.

CHAPTER 5

Chris and Lacey sat at a small outdoor table. The red market umbrellas shaded them from the warm sun, with no clouds in sight. As Melanie approached, Chris whistled. "Wow, don't you look gorgeous!"

Dropping her shoulders, Melanie glared. Deep inside, she appreciated the attention but wished that she didn't care so much. The wind picked up and blew her sundress. She quickly tamped it down.

"Man, Mel, that dress makes your beautiful green eyes pop!"

She glanced down at her flowy sage, floral print dress, regretting it as she heard Chris whistle. She tried ignoring him and noticed the table devoid of any dishes. "So, almost done?"

"Done? We just ordered," said Lacey.

Melanie opened her mouth to speak, but Chris interrupted.

"Okay, okay. Don't go all ballistic on me. Come on? How often do I get to spend time with my princess? Besides Mel, she wanted to go window shopping. Geez, look where we're at?" He flung his arms wide. "Beverly Hills! The girl couldn't resist."

"Oh, it's my fault?" Lacey smirked. "Thanks for throwing me under the bus, Chris."

Both Melanie and Chris swung around to face Lacey. "It's Dad," they said.

"I love it when you two do that!"

"Sit down, Mel. I'll order you a kale salad or something." He reached out to touch her hand.

Pulling away, Melanie stepped around and took a seat opposite Chris. She glared at him behind her shades and picked up the menu, signaling the server. "I'll have a cheeseburger, fries, and a chocolate shake, please."

"So, who is this woman, and what have you done with your mother?" Propping an elbow on the table, Chris rested his chin on a fist, ogling. "Go for it, girl!"

Avoiding his eyes, Melanie fidgeted. Finally, as the server turned to leave, Melanie blurted, "You know, on second thought, can you just make that a hamburger, no cheese, extra lettuce, and tomatoes and hold the mayo."

The server nodded.

"Oh, and never mind on the fries and milkshake. Just water, please."

"There's my girl." His teeth almost glistened in the bright sun.

She shivered. She preferred healthy food. Why did she let him get to her? "I'm not your girl, Chris." An awkward silence filled the air.

Lacey bit her lip, then said, too loudly, "So, Mom? How was the florist?"

A sweet, little bird flew across their table and landed at Chris's feet. Wearing loafers but no socks, he kicked at it.

"Dad, it's so cute," Lacey whispered.

"Shoo. Shoo. Go away!" He flapped his linen napkin.

Melanie stared. *How could I have ever fallen for him?* Back then, she was a foolish young girl, and she fell for the slightly older, handsome charmer. No one oozed charm like Chris.

"Mom? Hello, Mom?" Lacey yelled.

Chris stared back, and a corner of his mouth turned up, and he winked again.

She looked away as a familiar emptiness returned to her heart. She smiled at her daughter. "Good. I had a very productive morning."

The server brought the food, and Chris dug in. Lacey folded her hands and raised eyebrows towards Melanie.

"Hey, Chris, mind if we pray first?"

His mouth full, he wiped his lips and lowered his burger. "Sure, go ahead."

Melanie began to pray, but he interrupted with a whisper. "Still doing that, too, huh?"

A pang of sadness gripped her heart. Any inkling of faith made him uncomfortable. As she finished, she added a silent plea for him. Chris immediately began talking.

"So, ladies, I'm rolling in the dough now." He clapped his hands together. "I closed a couple of big deals, one down in San Diego and one here in LA. Heck, I might as well retire!"

"Retire? You're not even forty." *I should have sued for child support,* thought Melanie, but she never wanted his help. When he abandoned her, she wanted nothing to do with him. Yet here he was.

"Chris, you can't retire. You're not old enough. Grandpa's hardly retired!" exclaimed Lacey.

"Just temporarily. I'll start up when I feel like it. Besides, I'm going on an extended vacation to the Caribbean. Want to come, princess?"

"Yesss!"

Chris grimaced. "Oh, I'm sorry. Maybe not this time, sweetie, but …."

"No worries there, Chris. Lacey wasn't expecting a yes. We expect nothing from you." Melanie blew out a breath. *How could she be so mean, even to him?* Still, she burned inside, wishing she didn't wonder who he was taking with him on vacation.

Not that she really cared. She hurt more for her daughter. Like the bridal satin so easily torn, her heart ripped.

His soulful eyes widened, and he stared at his daughter. "I promise, princess. We'll plan a trip another time." He glanced at Melanie. "You can come too, but only if you'll be nice." A smile crept across his lips.

Touché, Melanie thought. *Touché, Chris.*

They finished their lunches, and Chris promised Lacey the moon as he slipped into his car and drove off. Lacey stood waving and hugged Melanie. "He's not all bad, you know?"

*No, he's not, but he's not right for me. If only…*the regrets returned. What could have been? Maybe not even so much for her, but for Lacey. A girl needed her father. Not that he was much of one. Either way, Melanie hated herself for wondering and asked God to take away the longing.

They climbed into her Mustang and breezed down the freeway towards home. Melanie watched the familiar landmarks fade by. The Porsche test track, the blimp, the power plants. All familiar on her long drives with Chris, long ago.

"Hey, mom? Can we go to Grandma and Grandpa's for dinner?"

"Dinner? We just had lunch."

Lacey made a puppy dog face.

Melanie chuckled. "Okay, I think that would be nice. By the time we get through rush hour, it'll be dinner time. Call them."

CHAPTER 6

"Mmm. Smells good, Grandma." Lacey ran into the kitchen of her grandparents' home. Melanie soaked in the scent from her mom's rose garden. Vivid shades of red, yellow, pink, and lavender. Her mom had so many colors and varieties. She was the envy of the neighborhood. Melanie reached down to the clippers lying next to the hose. She clipped a few stems and breathed in the sweet scent.

The screen door opened. "Hey, honey, come on in. Your mom's almost got dinner on the table." Her father took the flowers and shoved them in a vase already full of roses on the coffee table.

Rick always wore his baseball cap askew, smashing down his thick, light brown, barely gray hair. Melanie went in for an under-the-arm hug, relishing the coziness of his cotton shirt. The blue plaid matched his light eyes perfectly. The sound of a waltz greeted her, and she grabbed his hand and twirled herself under his arm. Taking her in his arms, he stepped lightly as they waltzed to The Blue Danube.

"One-two-two, one two-two...." Melanie counted as they spun around the room.

Tap. Tap. Melanie felt a light hand on her shoulder.

"May I?" Lacey cut in and took her grandfather's hand.

Rick swept Lacey in circles around and around the small living room.

"Hey, mom. Smells delicious." Melanie stepped into the kitchen and bent over the pot of beef stroganoff. Lifting the spoon, she touched her lips and slurped. "Mmm... My favorite." She walked over and hugged her mom.

"I know." Her mom nodded. "That's why I made it." Melanie towered over Patricia's petite frame. Her short graying hair a contrast to Melanie's long brown, sun-bleached waves.

Everyone sat at the table and joined hands. Rick nodded towards Lacey, and she prayed. The bowls of salad sitting in the middle of their plates indicated that it was the first course. Ever since Melanie could remember, she and Charlene weren't allowed to eat anything until they finished their salads first. That was her father's way of enforcing that she and her sister got their vegetables—a tiny remaining part of his old autocratic nature.

Lacey drenched her salad in ranch dressing while her grandfather piled high the cottage cheese. Melanie stood.

"What do you need?" asked Patricia.

"Just getting balsamic vinegar and olive oil."

"Oh, sorry, hon. I forgot." Patricia raised a hand and covered half her mouth. A loud whisper emitted from the other side. "Isn't that the same as Kraft Italian?" She chuckled.

"So, Mel, did you have time to look over the grant proposal?" Her father sounded hopeful.

"No." Melanie shrugged.

"Well, since they accepted our initial application, and I completed the financials, I thought you could get started on the business end of it."

"Just do it, Melanie. It'll make your father happy," said her mother.

"She means placate me." He playfully growled.

Lacey finished her salad and scooped up a pile of rice, and plopped it on her plate. She smothered it with the steaming beef stroganoff, and her plate was so full, it hid the delicate flowery design under all the sauce. Taking a huge spoonful, she closed her eyes and chewed away.

"Eat up, sweetie." Patricia pinched Lacey's chomping cheek.

"It's worth a shot," said Rick. "It's awful expensive to run a business here in California. Just thinking, it doesn't hurt to pursue all your options. After your meeting with the lawyer, it sounds like you could use a backup plan."

"All right, Dad. I'll look at it."

"Grandma, this is so good," Lacey mumbled with a mouth full.

Lacey was so engrossed in her food that she seemed oblivious to everything else. Both Patricia and Rick laughed. He then nodded at Melanie and winked as if to say, "We'll talk later."

After clearing the table, Melanie joined her father in the living room while Lacey and her grandmother washed dishes.

"Mel, how's the wedding planning going?"

"I have my biggest client yet. Remember last year I told you about the referral I got from that wedding I did at the winery in Silverado Canyon?"

He nodded.

"Well, that's coming up, and it's a big one."

"Bravo. That's my girl."

"Yeah. It must have been a God thing because this girl and her family are from Beverly Hills, and so is the groom." Melanie rubbed her thumb and fingers together, much like professional baseball players do when hitting a homerun and rounding the bases. "She could have gone with the biggest and best event planner in LA. I can't believe she chose me."

"You're better than the others. Don't sell yourself short.

That's why the bride chose you, and you said it. God gave this to you. Do your best, Mel, with the Lord's strength."

"Dad, this could be it. My name will get out there after this one. At least, I hope it will. With what I earn from this wedding and my savings, maybe I don't need Nina's inheritance or the grant after all."

Rick nodded, but his smile faded.

"Why is the grant so important to you? You think it's a sure thing?" Asked Melanie.

"No, not by a long shot. After we send in our proposal, it'll go before a board, and they'll compare it to the other applicants." He smoothed his hand across the worn green, velvet flowered sofa arm. "Then we'll wait and see what God does with it."

Faith had transformed her father, and she wasn't afraid of him anymore. Growing up, he'd been so stern and demanding. But all that changed, and she recalled the night Lacey was born. The night they reconciled.

His sorrowful brokenness over how he had treated Melanie when she'd gotten pregnant out-of-wedlock and the ensuing hasty wedding in Las Vegas was so long ago. She cringed, remembering how harshly she'd cut her parents off, but it was they who had made the first move to restore their relationship.

"I'd like you and the baby, Lacey, to come home." Rick had told her in the delivery room, and when he said her newborn daughter's name, she somehow knew things would turn out. Their prideful honor had fallen away, and her parents humbled themselves before God and the small family reunited.

Melanie's parents opened their home to their daughter and granddaughter without judgment. While Melanie agonized over losing Chris, she was happy raising Lacey with their help. Those times had been the brightest but often the loneliest of her life.

"All right. I'll do it."

Rick reached down to the old magazine rack aside the sofa. He pulled out a file of papers. "I was hoping you'd say that. Here you go. I did some research of my own to help you get started."

"So, Dad, why? Really? I know we have fond memories of Bay Town, but you and mom are here, and it's so far away."

"Who says we might not join you?"

Melanie's eyes grew round as saucers. "What?"

"Shhh."

"You never said you wanted to move back?" Melanie whispered.

"I never thought about it, but when this opportunity popped up, well... your mom and I aren't getting any younger, and life is too fast and too expensive here in Southern California. I know the south has their problems too, but it is a much slower pace."

"How so?" She wondered if he was just trying to convince her.

"They're not in a hurry down there. Why, just going to the grocery store here is frenetic. Everyone here is in a huff all the time, and the traffic? It's rush hour all the time. Don't get me worked up!"

She had to admit he was right, but the sun, the weather, the beach, those were the perks of living in So Cal. "Dad, you love Huntington Beach. Living in Surf City was always your dream. You made it. Retire at the beach, you said. If it hadn't been for you, I'd have no dreams. It's all you, Dad...."

Rick interrupted her. "Like you said..." he pointed upward, "A God thing. Anyway, you're a hard worker, Mel. Don't sell yourself short. And about moving? We'll cross that bridge when it comes. Perhaps I'm getting that itch to travel again."

Melanie's father got that right. He'd traveled all over the world. He lived on three different continents, five unique countries, three other states, and in more cities than he could count. Most of it was when he was a single man, but her sister Charlene and she had still benefited from traveling. They'd experienced some diverse cultures, and her mom, Patricia, loved the travel, too. It bonded them even more in their later years.

Still, Melanie asked. "How does mom feel about a move?"

"She loves adventure as much as I do, but she's just concerned about my...."

"Dessert! Who wants a banana split?" Lacey's yell interrupted their conversation.

"Worried about what, Daddy?"

Rick pushed off the sofa and stood. "Did you hear the girl? Come on before they eat it all."

"Are you serious? Didn't we already have ice cream this week?"

Lacey pointed to her grandmother, whose chin tipped downward. "Yes, we are serious. Chocolate syrup, strawberries, and pineapple. Whipped cream, nuts, and a cherry on top." She held up her prized cut-glass banana split boats for confirmation.

Strong hands rested on Melanie's shoulders. "Can't argue with that," said Rick.

CHAPTER 7

Sunday morning, Melanie and Lacey attended the first service at Faith Community. Though not an ancient building, the structure and layout were outdated. Retro, mid-century modern, some deemed it. A pulpit stood at the front, flanked by two fresh flower arrangements. This Sunday, perfumed gardenias filled the sanctuary. One wide aisle ran down the center, and lots of stained glass surrounded the room's perimeter as the sun glistened through the windows creating colorful prisms on the walls. Peace and serenity.

Seniors filled the pews, but a few of the younger crowd attended as well. The worship included hymns and responsive readings, and Melanie's spirit soared. This closeness to God probably had a lot to do with being closer to her parents, too.

Pastor Leland's message always inspired Melanie, and she took notes as he encouraged the congregation. She nodded, affirming that the difficulty came in the trials and challenges. Pastor Leland was an outstanding example of what it was to walk by faith. Experiencing life's tragedies made him a great counselor and a gifted pastor. He was a youthful fifty-five, and the congregation, both young and old, loved him.

As the service ended and the crowd filtered out, Pastor Leland stood outside, greeting everyone.

"Thank you so much, Pastor Leland. I loved your message."

Taking both of her hands in his, he squeezed. "God's message, Melanie, but I'm glad you liked it. Now go live it."

Patricia hugged him, and the girls drifted toward the coffee gazebo.

~

Melanie's father brought up the rear of the group.

Pastor Leland extended a hand. "Rick? How are you feeling these days?"

Rick furrowed his brow and raised a finger to his lips. "No need to worry the girls."

"Patricia's a strong woman, Rick. You should tell her."

"She knows a little. I'll share more when I need to. I hate for her to worry, and I'm fine." He lifted out a tiny vial from his pocket and dropped it back in. "Long as I have my nitro, I'm good."

Pastor Leland shook his head. "I'm praying for you, brother. Anything I can do or help with?"

"Nope. Doc said there is nothing more to do, so I'm taking it easy and enjoying my girls. Thanks, Pastor."

CHAPTER 8

The next morning, Melanie dressed in workout clothes and started the coffee. As she leaned back against the kitchen counter, she ignored the manila envelope with the grant application still sitting on the table and wrestled with her father's reasoning. Most people would die to live in sunny California.

Grabbing a handful of hair, she looked at the sun-bleached tips and pulled it back into a ponytail. Uncrossing her ankles, she placed both hands on the counter behind her and pushed off. The coffee had just finished brewing, and she poured a cup. The doorbell rang, and Melanie checked her watch. Lacey was showering, and it was too early for her carpool friend to show up. She strode to the door. As she opened it, a man's voice spoke.

"Hello, Mrs. Thompson?"

"Yes?" Melanie peered out and glanced down at the latched screen door.

"Sorry to bother you so early. You're Chris Thompson's wife, correct?" He didn't sound sorry.

A breath escaped. "I'm his Ex. Ex-wife. Why?"

"Is he home?"

"I'm sorry, who are you?" Melanie straightened. No one had ever come asking for Chris at her home. Ever.

"Just doing a background check. He works for us, and he gave this address."

This address? She doubted that Chris even knew where she lived. Melanie stared through the screen, wondering if the man looked familiar. He was easily overweight, even for his height, but his biceps bulged from the polo shirt he wore, and in contrast, a slight paunch hung over the waist of his athletic pants. Melanie observed that the clothes, though casual, were expensive. She glanced past him, but from the upstairs unit, she couldn't see the street. Her suspicions drove her courage. "Chris has never lived here. In fact, we hardly lived …Wait, what company did you say you were from?" Not that she knew where Chris worked. The less she knew, the better.

"Mom, do I have to drink this green smoothie?" Lacey yelled from the kitchen.

Before Melanie could answer, the man moved sideways and looked around her. He smiled. "That your daughter?"

Her eyes narrowed. "Who are you?"

The man slowly backed away. "Sorry. Just a mix-up." He chuckled, but it wasn't friendly. "Perhaps this was just a reference address." His body shook the balcony as he thundered down the stairs.

When Melanie was sure he was on the ground level, she pushed out the screen and stepped out onto the balcony. Gripping the wrought-iron railing, she leaned forward, watching him walk down the sidewalk and hoist himself into a large, black SUV, like the one on Saturday. Melanie questioned if this was the guy Chris argued with at the restaurant parking lot. She needed no more problems. Especially not his, and she didn't like the way this guy looked at Lacey. Something triggered in her heart, and Melanie decided. She had to let Chris go. It was time.

~

After dropping Lacey and her friend off at school, Melanie drove to her favorite beach trail, parked, and stepped out. Tying her light blue athletic shoes, she straightened up and tightened her ponytail, and her back went rigid. A black SUV pulled in a few spaces down. *Again?* Melanie stepped back between two cars. She stood, pretending to relax as she stretched. The door opened, and she held her breath, peeking out.

"Hi!" A woman about her age jumped from the SUV. She waved.

"Oh, hi."

"Great day for a run, huh?"

Melanie nodded and gave a sheepish grin, hating that she was so easily jarred. Not always, but sometimes she struggled with anxiety. Or, as her daughter called it, paranoia. *Whatever,* she thought, God always seemed to have her back. She just had to remember that.

Her ponytail swished as she jogged away, breathing a sigh of relief and feeling foolish for her paranoia. Crossing the railroad tracks, Melanie trekked down the dirt path that ran along the beach. The waves crashed loudly as the seagulls screeched overhead. She loved the beach, even the gritty sand, and noisy birds. Running the mile to the pier, she followed it out to the end, checked her watch, and did a U-turn. Some older fishermen tipped grimy baseball hats and waved as she jogged by. They reminded her of her father.

Twenty minutes later, she finished the three-mile run. Cooling down to a walk, she appreciated the beauty of swiftly moving clouds against a bright blue sky. Running took her mind off everything and placed it on God. Cross Country and Track in high school had gotten her started, and after Lacey was born, she'd taken it up again and never stopped. Besides the physical exercise, it cleared her mind. Just as she reached home, her cell beeped.

I'm in town. Can you meet for lunch? It was the bride for her upcoming booking.

Harper was a sweet amiable, and agreeable bride. Not at all anxious like most, and Melanie was so thankful. With what was going on in her life, a pleasant client was a gift. This was the biggest wedding she'd ever done, and everything had to be perfect. Harper made that easy.

After a quick shower and drying off, Melanie slipped on a simple form-fitting sleeveless dress—a light gray linen sheath with pin-hole white polka-dots. She reached for her taupe-colored sandals to complete the outfit. The vanity mirror reflected Melanie's fresh look. She lightly waved her hair and grabbed a handful from the top and sides. Twisting it back away from her forehead, she knotted it into a small bun. Applying light makeup, she finished with a light nude-colored gloss. Smacking her lips, she nodded to her reflection. *That will have to do.*

When Melanie arrived at the restaurant, she looked around. A stunning young woman with curly, long dark tresses waved. Her olive complexion glowed. "Hi, Melanie. You look adorable!"

Harper waved a perfectly polished nail up and down at her. She was shockingly gorgeous. A supermodel couldn't hold a candle to the beautiful goddess, but sitting across from her was a tall, demure, sweet-faced young woman. Blond and fair and just as beautiful as the bride. Either of them could be on the cover of Bride magazine.

"Thank you so much for meeting with me. I just needed you to calm my anxious heart!". Harper giggled. "Oh, this is Summer, my M-O-H."

"Maid of Honor, so nice to meet you, Summer."

The Cliff House was a five-star restaurant overlooking the Pacific Ocean. The view from the wooden deck displayed the crystal ocean with Catalina Island rising on the horizon. Harper motioned for Melanie to sit as she waved the server over. "More champagne, please, and a glass for my friend." She offered a palm toward Melanie.

"Oh, no, thanks. Iced tea, please."

"I get it. No drinking on the job." She giggled.

"No more for me, thank you very much. One glass is about all I can take." Summer drawled as she covered her glass with a delicate hand.

Her lilting voice intrigued Melanie. Ever since she had lived in the south as a young girl, southern accents mesmerized her. Some of her fondest childhood memories came from there. Her father had often expressed the same. "Summer, you're from the South?"

Harper laughed while placing her chin on clasped hands. Her elbows propped up on the small round table before them. "How could you tell?"

"Why, yes, ma'am. I'm originally from Mississippi, but my family resides in New Orleans now."

Before Melanie could respond, Harper spoke up again. "Summer is getting married too." Flipping back her hair, she looked between the two women. "Oh, Summer, let Melanie do your wedding. She's amazing!"

Melanie took a quick look at Summer's hand. The rock on her finger dazzled. The ring and diamond-studded bracelet practically blinded her.

"Maybe. We are having a long engagement, though. My beau is presently in law school," replied Summer.

"Well, whenever you're ready, I love the south, so I wouldn't mind flying down." Melanie's stomach lurched, and dollar signs rang up in her head at the cost of commuting to coordinate everything. Still, when she envisioned planning a lovely southern wedding, the idea of being featured in Southern Bride Magazine emblazoned across her brain.

I'm getting ahead of myself. Melanie blinked and turned her attention to Harper. "Well, let's finish up the details of your special day, shall we?"

CHAPTER 9

After lunch, Melanie went straight to the shop. Gloria and Tito greeted her. "Hey, we need to talk," said Gloria.

Tito and Gloria followed Melanie to her office. Tito's short, round body squeezed into the club chair opposite Melanie's desk, his laptop propped over his knees. Gloria's chair touched his, and she attempted to scoot away. The cramped office afforded little room to move, and Melanie hadn't had time to redecorate. Fabric swatch books spilled from the desk to the floor. A dress rack stuffed with dress samples crowded a corner, and a large, cluttered bulletin board with ripped-out magazine pictures and outstanding orders encased in plastic sleeves covered the wall behind Melanie. Even the workstation with printer/fax took up a corner. Not exactly the dream office she'd envisioned.

"Did you see they're gearing up to tear down some of the buildings on the street?" said Tito.

"The demolition is starting." Gloria nodded.

"What are you talking about? I saw nothing." Melanie stared back.

"In the alley," Tito pointed over his shoulder. "A bulldozer and a crane with a wrecking ball are parked back there."

"For what?"

"The takeover! Why do you think the landlord's trying to get you out? He's selling these buildings to some big developer." Tito threw his hands up.

Tito told the women he overheard some construction workers talking at the food trucks. Good at asking the right questions, he found out that the other shops had sold out, and since Nina's bridal shop was right smack in the center of the block, she was holding things up.

"I'll call Mr. Randall," said Melanie.

"Do you have the money to fight this?" asked Gloria.

"I'm not sure if I should. I never thought of this option before, but what if we just sold the business?"

"It's your call. Heck, I'm ready to retire, anyway," shrugged Gloria.

Melanie looked at Tito. "And you?"

"I'm part-time. I can pick up another gig pretty easily. Accountants, good ones like me, are in high demand."

A knock was followed by a sales associate peeking in the doorway. "Sorry to bother you, but I just signed for this registered letter."

Melanie took it. "Not again. It's from the landlord." As she read, her eyes widened. "Are you kidding me? This is an offer to buy out our business." She handed the letter to Tito.

His eyes moved back and forth across the pages. "This isn't an offer. It's a rip-off! He's giving you twenty-four hours to decide? Tell him to forget it."

"I'm telling you. The guy wants you out. When you turn it down, the fight begins," said Gloria.

"There's going to be a fight either way." Melanie felt herself flush, and a light sweat broke out across her forehead. "What are my options? If I refuse the offer, we have to move, or I need to hire an attorney to fight the eviction."

"Do we have the money to move?" Gloria looked at Tito. "What's cheaper?"

Tito closed his laptop. "I'd guess the move, but then we have to find a building. Rents will be higher wherever we go."

"How much is a lawyer?" asked Gloria.

"Mr. Randall said he could recommend one, but it would cost $1000 initially and up to $400 an hour after."

Tito clasped his hands behind his head. "I'm in the wrong business."

"What can we afford, Tito?"

"Not that." He opened his laptop again, his fingers flying. "We can make cuts everywhere, but it won't be enough."

"I'll call Mr. Randall. Gloria, can you scan this letter and email it to him?"

"Sure." She picked up the letter and left. Tito followed.

Within a few minutes, Gloria handed Melanie the letter. "Here you go."

Melanie put a call into her lawyer and stared at her cell phone lying on her desk. She listened to nothing as she waited for Mr. Randall to speak. She sat with her elbows propped on the arms of her desk chair, tapping her fingers together, wondering what he thought of the letter she sent over.

"This is a low-ball offer, isn't it?" His voice rang through her cell phone speaker, and Melanie leaned forward. "I looked over your lease again, and although it's not my expertise, the way the lease is written, you might have a chance if you fight it." Mr. Randall paused. "I will tell you this, though. I did some research, and the lawyer who sent this letter, the one representing the owner, he is not very reputable."

"What do you mean?" The shaved-headed driver popped into Melanie's brain.

"They have connected him with some crimes committed against other tenants. Well, not him, but his client."

"What kind of crimes?"

"Break-in, vandalism, threats, harassment. Nothing life-threatening, but serious all the same. The charges were filed against his client, the building owner, but they were all dropped. It's important that you're aware."

Melanie drew a deep breath and nodded.

After she'd finished her call, she sat, staring at the offer. It was a ridiculous offer, and twenty-four hours wasn't enough time to decide. If she didn't accept the offer, they still couldn't evict her immediately. She had at least two more months of extension, but the sixty days brought her no consolation as dark thoughts clouded her mind. *Crimes, he had said.*

Melanie picked up her cell and called her sister. "Hey, Char. I need to run something by you."

Melanie and her sister Charlene shared a closeness that kept them tied by phone or text.

"Sure, sis. What's up?" Charlene sounded cheery.

Melanie told her about the eviction and the offer.

"What a creep! Yeah, don't hire an attorney yet, but fax me the lease agreement. I'll see if someone in our legal group can help. They owe me some favors. If nothing else, we can send letters to that slum lord. Let the jerk know he can't push you around."

Melanie smiled at Charlene's choice of words. Her sister was at her best fighting bad guys, and Charlene worked for a non-profit that battled against human injustice. She was an activist in every sense of the word but would challenge anyone who labeled her as such.

"Thanks for your help, sis. I didn't know who else to call. I didn't want to bother Daddy."

"You got that right. Don't get him all worked up. We'll handle it. You're strong, girl! So, what else is new?"

Melanie leaned back in her chair, taking the time to fill Charlene in on her life. She told her about Chris calling and coming around more of late. Charlene was less than happy. Melanie also mentioned the incident with the man at her door.

"That Chris. What a weasel. The nerve of him giving out your address." Charlene got more worked up over the stuff Chris did than the man at Melanie's door.

"Well, Chris has left on an extended vacation, so he's out of the picture for now." Still, Melanie hesitated. "So, you don't think it's anything?"

"Nah. Sounds legit to me. Except a phone call would be more normal. Anyway, that's pretty nervy that Chris would list you as a referral. Even for him. You were probably the only stable thing in his life." Charlene laughed. "Well, you could have been. You guys were pretty wild back then. I'm sure glad you let him go. Good move, sis." Charlene wasn't the only one fighting a grudge against Chris.

Her sister's tirade lightened Melanie's burden. "Well, I'm doing a very important wedding soon."

"That's great. I bet Dad's proud of you." Charlene's voice went soft. "Hey, how is he?"

"What do you mean? Haven't you talked to him lately? You guys get into a political fight or something?" Melanie teased.

"Nah. Dad just doesn't get as warm and fuzzy with me like he does you. No biggie."

"Would you want him to? You're like a porcupine to everybody." Melanie chuckled.

"Yeah, maybe so."

The sadness in Charlene's voice hit Melanie's heart. "Charlene, Daddy loves you, you know that. No different from me."

The girls were half-sisters, and although Rick was not Charlene's biological father, he had loved her as his own right from birth. Still, their relationship was a bit strained, and it wasn't until Charlene was living back east that God had made life changes in Rick, resulting in a more compassionate father. Melanie benefitted firsthand, but Charlene from a distance.

"I know that sis. Sometimes it's hard not to blame every little nuance on the past. Anyway, is he okay? He's getting up there in age."

"He's fine, but he's all wrapped up in me applying for the grant in Mississippi." Melanie had told her sister about it in their last phone call. "He's pretty insistent, too. I don't get it."

"Backup plan. That's Dad. Besides, you'd be closer to the east coast and closer to me. Anyway, I talked with mom the other day. She seems good. So, how's my girl?"

Melanie smiled. "Lacey's doing great."

"Good. She's a great kid. Give her a hug for me. Listen, I have to run. I have a meeting."

The sisters said their goodbyes, and as Melanie hung up, she wished Charlene didn't live so far away. Well, there was another point in Mississippi's favor. It was much closer to Charlene.

Melanie finished her work, picked up Lacey, and headed home. "We still have time for a jog, Lacey. Want to join me?" She turned into the apartment complex.

"What about dinner?" Lacey asked. She was always hungry.

"How about I go for a run, and you make us a healthy salad? I have some cooked chicken in the fridge. We're all set."

"Uh, how about I just make some spaghetti?" Lacey licked her lips.

"Whatever."

As the girls trudged the concrete steps to their upper unit, a neighbor greeted them.

"Hey, girls. What's up?" The guy's bright smile often shined a light on Melanie's day, but she worked hard at ignoring it. Ever since Chris, the only relationship she thought about investing in was her daughter.

She guessed he was her age and probably single. He lived alone but had friends over at least weekly. It was a quiet group, but she often heard singing. Whenever Melanie greeted him in passing, he always made friendly conversation.

"Hey. Not much. How's it going?" Lacey asked.

"Good." He shrugged. "Better make sure your garage and cars are locked. There were a couple of thefts in the alley, and the girl in unit A downstairs had a phone stolen from her car." A quick smile, and he nodded. "Hey, I'm running to the store. Need anything?"

"No. No, thanks."

He's so nice, thought Melanie. She hadn't dated since Chris, but occasionally, a kind, friendly man caught her attention. Smiling at Lacey, she shrugged. That part of her life was on pause. She reminded herself.

Melanie unlocked the door, and stepping into her apartment, she breathed deep. Every corner and window in the living room and kitchen overflowed with plants. The greenery, all in various sized white pots, brought peace and calm to her busy life. Unlike most people her age, she loved more traditional furnishings, and a few antique reproductions dotted the room.

The girls dropped their bags, and Lacey flopped on the white sofa. Melanie changed into her running clothes.

"Lock the door. I'll be back in thirty."

The sun had already set, but the evening glow hovered, lighting the night sky. Streetlights lit the way, and Melanie turned into the park. She scrolled her phone and turned on the music app. Listening to Christian praise and worship music always helped to put her spirit right. The creamy-yellow star-shaped flowers hanging beneath the Linden tree branches distracted her as she drank in the powerful perfume. A blend of honey and lemon peel permeated the park, soothing her somewhat.

She jogged about a half-mile before she realized that the overgrown trees had made the path dark, and angst arose. The last song ended on her playlist, and she stopped to click it off and headed home. Whenever she jogged, by the end of the playlist, she was ready to do some thinking. Usually, it was to work out issues plaguing her brain at the close of the day. Today, she had many.

As she exited the park, she saw a flicker of light down the street. She squinted her eyes and saw smoke filtering from the window of a parked car. It was too dark to see much, but she noticed someone sitting inside. Ignoring an uncomfortable feeling in her stomach, she jogged home. Hearing an engine, she turned slightly and saw the car pull from the curb, following her. The car sped up, and she ran faster. It was close, and she felt the rumble of the engine. Just as it swerved towards her, she jumped on the curb. One foot made it, the other twisted, and she fell. The car stopped. A bald man exited the vehicle.

"Help!" She screamed and struggled to stand. Her ankle pulsed with pain. She limped towards the driveway to her apartment complex, but she couldn't move fast enough as the man approached. *Oh, God, please,* she prayed.

"Hey! Are you all right?" A voice came from the apartment parking lot, and a shadow approached her. It was her neighbor.

The bald man stopped. A slight shadow of fuzz covered the shaved head.

"What happened? I heard a scream." Her neighbor wrapped an arm around her waist and helped her up.

"Him." She pointed. "He almost ran me over!"

The man with the shaved head yelled over his shoulder. "You're crazy, lady." Before he slid into his car, he turned and yelled. "Seems like you have a problem with curbs." He laughed and sped off, but not before the neighbor clicked a picture of the car.

"I'm calling the police."

Melanie covered his hand with hers. "No. I'll handle it." But her knees buckled.

Strong hands caught her, and Melanie leaned into him for a moment. She closed her eyes and took deep breaths. His strength felt good, but a moment later, she pulled away as his hands still steadied her.

"Are you sure? Did you get his license plates? I probably got a blurry photo at best."

Melanie shivered and pulled away. "It's a long story." *Maybe not so long.* Everything had been happening so fast, but now she had an idea of what was going on. The landlord meant business. He wanted her out.

"Thank you …" She couldn't recall the neighbor's name. She couldn't remember ever knowing it. "What were you doing here?"

"I just got back from the store." He smiled. "Perfect timing, huh? You really think he tried to hit you? Shouldn't we report this?"

"Like I said, it's a long … actually it's a short story, but no thanks." Still, she wondered if maybe she should call the police.

Melanie took a step and winced. His hands steadied her, and the support felt good as they walked back to the apartments. The flight of stairs would have been difficult without his arms hoisting her up each step.

"Are you sure you're okay?" He wasn't much taller than her, but his muscled arms steadied her as he gripped her waist. His kind eyes and sweet smile caused her to flush. She caught him staring back at her, and he quickly dropped his hand.

"I'll be fine, really."

"Well, if you ever need to talk, I'm here." His smile was comforting.

"Thanks." Melanie knew she'd never take him up on it, but the offer warmed her inside.

"Well, I have to go to a meeting. I'll see you later." He ran down the stairs and stopped at the bottom. "I still think you should report the guy."

"Maybe." Melanie smiled but wondered what kind of meeting. She looked at her watch. Did he go to rehab meetings? Damaged goods, she thought, but a check in her spirit caused a rapid confession of judgment, and she said a quick prayer for him.

CHAPTER 10

Melanie limped inside and leaned against the closed door. She looked at Lacey, pouring over her homework. Sweet, quiet Lacey. What if it had been her?

"I'm taking a shower."

"Uh, huh." Lacey never looked up.

Melanie limped to her room and phoned the police. She reported what happened, but they said nothing much could be done without a name and no license plate number. When she insisted it was a genuine threat and recounted a similar incident at the crosswalk, they transferred her to a detective. He took the report, gave her a case number, and told her to call if she had any more concrete evidence. She wasn't too hopeful, but tenseness oozed out, and she relaxed a little. At least she'd done something.

Melanie looked at her watch and pinched the bridge of her nose. Her shoulders tightened again. She had less than twenty-four hours to refuse or accept the offer to purchase her business. The time ticked away, and she couldn't help but wonder what the landlord would do next.

When she returned to the kitchen, Lacey stared. "What's with the limp?"

"Oh, I twisted my ankle on my run. No big deal." She

almost choked on her words, and the girls quietly ate their dinner.

Melanie swirled her spaghetti around her fork and brooded over the new events in her life. She struggled to fight the rising anxiety from the evening.

"What's up, Mom?"

"Nothing. Why?"

"Why so quiet?"

"Just tired, sweetie." Melanie forced a smile.

After they finished, Lacey cleared the table, kissed her mom, and retreated to her room.

Opening the freezer, Melanie reached for an ice pack. Sitting in a kitchen chair, she raised her leg and rested it on another chair. The ice pack cooled her sore ankle. If only it could fix everything. These guys meant business. *Was it worth it? What if they came after Lacey?* She seriously contemplated liquidating and closing the shop. But how would that affect the other employees? She considered moving costs versus hiring an eviction lawyer. The latter wouldn't prevent incidents like tonight. It would be a sleepless night. She needed to pray.

The following day, Melanie's ankle felt better until she tried on dress shoes, and her swelled joint pulsed. Changing her outfit, she went casual and wore flat shoes.

As she drove to the office, a thought occurred to her. She'd never mentioned to the police that she thought the man who attempted to hit her was connected to the landlord. She called the police again. Melanie pulled out the business cards of the landlord and his lawyer, and she reported them both. It wasn't five minutes later that she got a call from a detective. He told her that others were harassed, too, by the same man, and she was instructed to report anything suspicious. He promised to follow up.

The detective had fueled her courage, and she made another call. She would refuse the landlord's offer to buy her out. Staying there was no longer an option, but she would never sell to him. She dialed the lawyer's number and refused the offer.

"Mrs. Thompson. You should reconsider," said the lawyer. Now he really sounded like *Michael Corleone.*

"No. I shouldn't. Did you know your driver tried to kill me last night?"

"I don't know what you're talking about."

"I reported him to the police. Your client tried to run me down twice."

"That wasn't my cli…." He didn't finish.

"How do you know it wasn't? Oh, the guy with the shaved head is just your hitman, right?"

The lawyer chuckled. "That's a little dramatic, don't you think?"

"The detective at the police station didn't seem to think so."

Silence on the other end.

"I gave his description, and I have a picture of the silver car." Melanie didn't tell him that the photograph wasn't identifiable. "The detective was very interested."

More silence.

"Oh, and I do have a legal team. They'll be contacting you shortly." He didn't need to know it was a non-profit legal team, thanks to Charlene. Feeling like she was winning, Melanie continued. "I was told the grounds for eviction are weak. Besides, you can't do anything about the three-month extension."

She heard his throat clear. "Mrs. Thompson, I'll be frank. We need you out of the building as soon as possible. Let's not make this any more difficult than need be. I'll have another offer for purchase by tomorrow. Please reconsider."

"I will if it's a considerable amount higher." Melanie smiled and pulled down a fist while silently hissing, "Yes!"

∼

Weeks passed, and the new offer never came, and neither did any more incidents. The detective had paid a visit to the landlord, and Charlene's legal aid had written letters. Lately, Melanie's life was uneventful, and it gave her time to think about what she wanted. She could put the business on the market, but would it sell in a couple of months? Moving seemed to be the best option, but it would be costly and eat up her savings. Her heart's desire was still to own a storefront wedding consulting service, and this whole bridal shop was interfering.

The time was right for a change in plans, and the decision was solely hers. She never told her father about the frightening incidents, so she couldn't talk to him. Either way, she needed more money. That was what propelled her decision to apply for the business loan, just in case.

The initial meeting with the loan officer at the bank went well. Melanie was encouraged, but the tedious paperwork bogged her down. By the time she got it all together—the application, the financials, and the business plan—she was ready to throw in the towel. Melanie wished she could have run it by her father, but she'd resolved to do this on her own, and she did. When the bank contacted her to discuss her application, she was confident and ready. The butterflies in her stomach told her otherwise, but she made an appointment, and before she knew it, the day arrived.

"Well, Mrs. Thompson. This business plan looks very impressive. You certainly know a lot about servicing clients." The friendly loan officer ruffled through the papers.

Melanie brushed back her already smooth hair. Tightly banded in a ponytail, the style accented her polished and professional look. "Thank you. I've been in the industry for fifteen years."

"Yes, that's wonderful. Experience is an enormous factor. Successful experience." The woman nodded her approval. "Can you tell me a little about that?"

"Sure. I started as a receptionist and worked my way up. In fact, I've inherited that same shop."

"That's a huge plus in your favor, and I see you've listed that in your assets. So, you would need this loan to expand the business, or what exactly did you have in mind?"

"Well, yes, I guess so." Her confidence waned. This loan was a security blanket for an unknown future.

The loan officer waited, but Melanie bit her lip, and her mind went blank.

"All right then, let's move on. One obstacle is collateral. I see you're renting an apartment. Do you own any real estate?"

"I don't."

"Except for the bridal shop?"

"Actually, I don't own the building. It's leased." Melanie's stomach knotted. This was bad. Even the lease was in jeopardy.

"Oh, I missed that. Can you get a co-signer with collateral for this loan?"

"I can, but…."

"It would help substantially. I can submit the loan application as is, but without collateral or a co-signer, loan approval will be difficult."

Melanie felt like she'd been sucker-punched. *Maybe she would ask Charlene for help or even Chris. Definitely not her dad.* She nodded and said a silent prayer. "I understand, but what you have there is all me, and I would like you to submit it as is."

She smiled. "All right, let's submit it." Her words somehow encouraged Melanie.

"Thank you so much."

"My pleasure, Mrs. Thompson. With any luck, let's see if we can get this loan approved."

∾

The big wedding day arrived. The rustic wedding site in Malibu Canyon was perfect for Harper and her groom, and it played out like a dream. The bride's grand entrance in a white horse-drawn carriage drew applause. With the setting sun, the night lights entwined around trees and trellises, the fairy tale setting sparkled. Night-blooming jasmine drenched the air with its sweet aroma. A trill of a solo flute escorted the beautiful bride down the aisle to her handsome groom. Melanie reveled in the results of her efforts.

After the ceremony, the dining and dancing moved to the open area beyond the massive old oak trees. As Melanie walked through the crowd checking on Harper's details, the bride caught her eye from across the lawn. Harper waved and blew Melanie a kiss. A familiar scene at most weddings she planned. Melanie waved back and perused the grounds. Spotting the maid of honor, Summer, Melanie hoped for a consultation appointment. It was a long shot, but the way things were going, she might spring for that trip to Mississippi. Heck, her father could even join her! But Summer simply nodded a sweet smile.

The day after the wedding, Melanie propped her feet on the railing and wiggled her toes, sitting on her front balcony. Holding up a bottle of sparkling water, she raised it high. "Thank you, Jesus!" Elation still swelled after a job well done. Melanie breathed deep.

The house phone rang, interrupting her little celebration. Only her parents called on the landline. She walked into the house and answered it. Melanie scowled at the phone. "Mom?... Wait…Slow down. Where are you?"

Lacey emerged from her bedroom and stepped closer.

"Is he okay? Text me the address. I'm on my way."

Lacey's eyes widened, and she leaned in, pushing her ear close to Melanie's.

"Are you sure? ... Well, make sure you stay the night then and don't let Daddy drive tomorrow. Call me when you get home. Love you, give Daddy our love. Bye."

"What's wrong with Grandpa?" Lacey asked.

She took Lacey's hand. "He had some chest pains, and they stopped at an urgent care. He spent a few minutes with the doctor. Your grandfather can be so stubborn sometimes. Mom said after fifteen minutes, he walked out, and the doctor said he could go home. They're staying the night in Santa Barbara and will be back tomorrow evening."

"Will he be okay?" Lacey's voice shook.

Melanie wrapped her arm around her daughter. "Mom said he's got some heart issues that he's not telling us about." She breathed deep and smiled, but inside, she begged God to keep her dad and mom safe. Melanie pulled her daughter close. "Hey, let's go to evening church."

The packed pews felt somehow empty without Rick and Patricia. After the service, Melanie and Lacey waited in line to greet Pastor Leland.

"Are your parents coming home tonight?"

Melanie gave him a sideways glance. "Did Mom call you?"

"She did." He held Melanie's hand tightly and patted her shoulder. "She asked for prayer. Your dad will be fine. He knows how to take care of himself."

"What do you mean?"

His eyes widened, and Pastor Leland looked like she caught him with his hand in the cookie jar. "You know, we're getting older, and our bodies are wearing down."

"He's twenty years older than you." An inkling told her he was holding something back, but she pressed her lips tightly.

"I'm not so sure my father is taking care of himself."

"Well, if he gives you any trouble, call me. I'll straighten him out," he chuckled.

"Thanks, I'll do that." She pointed a finger at him. "I'm holding you to it."

"My pleasure, Melanie."

His voice soothed her, but the burden she carried seemed to build.

Melanie and Lacey settled in at home after church. After a quick dinner, they watched an old black and white movie, ate popcorn, and cuddled on the sofa. When the movie ended, Lacey kissed her mom goodnight and retreated to her room. Melanie locked up, but she still wasn't ready for sleep. She turned on the tea kettle and walked to the living room, peeking out the curtains. It was a pleasant neighborhood, and she'd been fortunate to find the place in her price range. Still, a nagging pulled in her brain. Her business, the landlord, her father, what was God doing?

A heaviness hung in her heart and on her mind. Someone to talk to would be nice right about now. She thought of the neighbor. The likable guy who offered his help, but what could he do? A reassuring presence if she needed it, maybe. A thought crossed her mind. *I could invite him for a cup of decaf.* She looked at her pajamas and banished the thought. What if he thought she was making a move on him or something? She chuckled, not even knowing how to do that.

Melanie walked past the manila envelope as she headed towards the whistling teapot. Turning off the flame, she placed two chamomile tea bags in her favorite mug and poured the water. She cupped her hands around her hot mug and took a sip. The evening wasn't cold, but the heat of the ceramic comforted her. Her eyes rested on the manila envelope, and she reached for it.

The financials were thorough. Rick had put himself as co-owner, which boosted her credibility. Melanie smirked. He'd co-sign for this but not the bank loan. Not that she asked.

He had researched every detail, even the schools. *Would Lacey mind the move?* Then she thought about Chris. Part of her was glad that his visits had been limited to once a year, but things were changing, and Lacey liked his increased interest. The flutter in Melanie's stomach triggered her feelings again. She really didn't want him in her life again, of that she was sure. An ache twisted in her belly. He still pulled at her heartstrings, and that could never be a good thing. *Maybe a move would be good.*

Melanie plopped down and pulled her tablet from her bag. She pulled up the business plan that she'd written for the bank, saved a new copy, and made changes that would work for the grant. After many attempts at the correct wording, she closed the laptop and stretched.

Peeking in on Lacey, Melanie found her flat on her back, arms sprawled outward. Lacey was sound asleep. She stepped to the bedside, lifted a Bible off Lacey's chest, and placed it on the nightstand. As she pulled up the covers, she tucked them close around Lacey's neck and kissed her forehead. *Thank you, God.*

CHAPTER 11

A week later, when Melanie's parents rested up from their road trip, they invited Melanie and Lacey for a barbecue. Corn-on-the-cob, burgers, salad, watermelon, and chips were the standard fare for outdoor food. And in California, summer food worked year-round.

After dinner, Lacey pulled at her grandmother's hand and pointed to the garden. They got up, and Patricia shared with Lacey all about the new plants she'd foraged from the neighborhood. Notorious for taking a pair of scissors on her evening walks, she always returned with a handful of fresh clippings to plant.

The garden held happy memories. Lacey grew up here. Her parents had been hers and Lacey's entire lives. Melanie had been so busy working and raising Lacey that she didn't really forge a life of her own. Still, she couldn't be happier with the joy of her parents being so close. They did everything together—movies, game nights, even vacations. She felt blessed, but a sadness arose as she stared at her father.

"So? What's with your heart, Daddy?"

He blew out a long breath. "I'm fine, Melanie."

"You're not fine. You went to Urgent Care on your trip. What was it, and how long has this been going on?"

"I have chest pains occasionally. The doctor gave me some nitroglycerin tablets, and if I must, I take them. That's it. I manage."

"What causes your pain, Daddy?"

"Melanie, I said I manage, and I mean it. It's not your concern. Trust me on this."

"I do trust you, but——"

He raised a palm. "No buts. It's not up for discussion."

She'd heard that tone before, but not in a long time. Melanie picked up the soiled paper plates and walked to the trash can. She tossed them in and slammed on the lid.

Her father sat back in his lawn chair, aside from the redwood picnic table. He smiled and looked happy, staring at Lacey and Melanie's mom. Melanie followed his gaze and glanced around the yard. Nothing matched in their back-yard, but somehow the eclectic mix of furniture, potted orchids, and hanging plants added to the family comfort of home.

"So, Mel, did you finish the grant proposal?" Rick acted as they'd never talked about his health.

"I did. But now that the wedding with the Beverly Hills client is over, I have some clout here." She rattled off with excitement about all the details and the expenses of the enormous event. "And you know, Dad, I'm getting some interest and consultations." Her enthusiasm spilled out.

"That's great, honey." He pushed up his glasses. "But anything could happen, you know."

"Like what?" She didn't feel like going over this again, especially after she'd already applied for the bank loan without him knowing. "Dad, it's not like I'm going to move to Mississippi, so it makes little sense."

She didn't like seeing his jaw set and watched as he drew a deep breath.

"You know, Mel, it's awfully expensive living here in Southern California, and prices keep escalating. Small businesses are closing up left and right. Now might be a good time to consider moving."

"You said that, but Dad, I'm not going anywhere without Mom and you. The beach has always been your dream. I know you said you'd consider moving but come on."

"I'm serious. I might consider moving if it means a better life for you and Lacey. A better future. Besides, you loved living in Bay Town." He tipped his baseball cap back. "It couldn't be more than a coincidence that's who's offering the grant."

His insistence was grating. "You don't believe in coincidences. And Daddy, my life is better because of you. despite my stupid mistakes."

He narrowed his eyes and glanced over at Lacey.

"I didn't mean Lacey. You know that. She's the best thing that ever happened to me." Melanie's heart warmed as a smile broke out across her father's face. "So, quit talking about a better life for us. We'll make it. Don't you always say to trust God?"

He nodded and reached over, patting her hand. "Did I ever tell you how proud I am of you? You've done well, Melanie."

Warmth rose, and she felt her face flush. It meant the world to her to hear those words. "Thanks, Dad." She stood and kissed his cheek. "Oh, and I sent the proposal off. I don't get it, but if it makes you happy...."

"It does, Mel. It gives me something to look forward to, and I'll be praying for it."

"But what if we're praying for two different things?"

"Well, like I said, it's all in God's strength. We just have to trust Him, and He'll show us the way, won't he?" His cool blue eyes shined.

"Melanie?" Patricia's voice rose from the far end of the yard.

"Coming!"

Her mother and Lacey were standing in the raised bed along the back wall, both trying to move an enormous pot holding a leafy Ficus.

"What in the world are you doing?" asked Melanie.

"Grandma doesn't like this spot anymore." Lacey tugged.

Melanie wedged between them, and together the three tugged, but it wouldn't budge.

"Not happening, Mom."

Rick came out. "Need another hand?"

Patricia and Melanie immediately yelled, "No!"

"Move over," Rick said.

Being compliant, Melanie shifted but caught her mother's face.

"No, Rick. It's okay. We'll leave it here." Patricia insisted. "The roots probably went deep."

"Oh, come on. The four of us can wiggle it out. Let's go on the count of three. One, two, three."

They all heaved, and the pot stayed put. Lacey sputtered as leaves brushed her face. She stood up straight. "Sorry, Grandma. No way this baby is moving."

"You're right. Come on. Time for dessert."

Everyone stepped out of the bed and retreated to the house—everyone except Rick.

Before stepping in the backdoor, Melanie heard a moan. She turned and saw her father hunched over, hanging on to the gnarled trunk of the Ficus tree. He clutched his chest.

"Daddy!" Melanie ran over to support his declining frame.

Lacey and Patricia followed.

Patricia screamed. "Rick! Rick!"

"Daddy, what's wrong? Lacey, call 911."

Rick slid to the ground but raised his hand, appearing to wave off Lacey. Instead, he reached for his pocket. Melanie was quicker and pulled out a small bottle.

"What's this?" She read the bottle. "You need nitro?" Melanie's hushed voice breathed out the words.

He nodded toward her hand, and she opened the vial. With tears brimming, Melanie asked, "How many?"

"One." He whispered. "Hurry."

Rick popped the tiny white pill into his mouth and slumped against Melanie. Patricia kneeled by his side, sobbing, and Lacey sat wide-eyed, hugging them both. With his eyes closed, he slumped in the dirt, surrounded by his family.

The paramedics arrived, and Rick was already recovering. The nitro worked, and he insisted on staying home against the paramedic's recommendation to hospitalize him. Patricia's insistence was greater. She was a force not to be reckoned with, so off he went. He was admitted, they ran tests, and fortunately, he didn't have a heart attack, just severe angina, again, but Patricia stayed with him just the same.

Melanie and Lacey's drive home was silent. Lacey juggled to balance three small pots on her lap.

Finally, Melanie spoke, attempting to lighten the tenseness. "So, what are you going to do with all those plants?"

"I'll probably kill them." Lacey's voice whined. "Grandma keeps giving me her clippings. I have so many empty pots. You could probably do wedding favors for a hundred guests." Her bangs flew up with the gust from her lips.

They both laughed, and the somber mood lifted somewhat.

"Well, we won't tell her, will we?"

Lacey's laugh faded, and her young voice took a serious tone. "Mom? What will happen to Grandpa?"

"Well, I'm calling Charlene. She'll handle Dad." Melanie's nod did little to affirm her statement.

"But really, Mom." Lacey's voice was almost a whisper.

"They'll release him tomorrow. He didn't suffer heart damage, so that's good. We can thank God for that. But he needs to take it easy."

I wish he would have told us. So many thoughts swirled. Melanie was thankful that she hadn't asked her dad to co-sign for her bank loan. And the move to Mississippi? That wasn't even a consideration anymore.

"Anyway, Lacey, I called Pastor Leland, and the church is praying for him." She glanced at her daughter. "Keeping him down will be the hard thing."

Lacey nodded. "You got that right. Poor Grandma."

"Poor Grandpa!" Melanie added.

Rick recovered slowly. He was still reluctant to share his complete condition, though it didn't stop Melanie and Patricia from prodding. He told them he had things under control. Melanie was just worried about any other underlying factors. Charlene had flown in for a quick visit to see for herself and got nowhere in finding out how serious his heart condition was. Life was in a holding pattern with her dad's health, but they needed to learn to navigate.

The bridal shop was doing well, and the hefty fee from the Malibu wedding increased Melanie's bank account. An added plus was an unexpected phone call. It was from Summer, the maid of honor from the wedding she did in Malibu.

"Yes. Hi, Summer." Melanie perked up. "It's good to hear from you. How's Mississippi?"

"Hot and sticky. That's why I'm heading to your neck of the woods." A lilted laugh filled the air like sweet music. "Well, not woods, but beach. Listen, I'll be in town to visit Harper." Her southern drawl was beautiful, and every word gave Melanie hope. "Anyway, I'd like to consult with you about my wedding."

"Oh! Congratulations. Did you set a date?"

"Yes, we did. Will you be available for a meeting next month? May we do lunch?"

"Sure, that would be great. Let's do that."

With the appointment made, a dart hit Melanie's heart,

and she wondered if it was the right timing to take a booking where the wedding would be held across the country in Mississippi. Her whole life felt upside down right now.

~

A few more weeks passed, and Melanie felt like it was the calm before the storm. Driving to the shop with the top down, Melanie pushed back her hair, but the wind whipped it around. She laughed, and for the moment, she imagined away all her problems. That was until she arrived at her shop, where the black and white squad cars were scattered in front. Shattered glass covered the sidewalks. The front windows had a huge gaping, jagged hole, and Gloria stood outside, hand over her brow.

"Gloria! What happened?" Melanie yelled after jumping from her car.

Gloria tried to speak, but the police interrupted. "What's your name, please?"

"Melanie Thompson."

"She's the owner." Gloria squinted.

Melanie's shoulders slumped at the mess. Wedding party mannequins lay knocked down inside the shop. "What happened?"

"I was dressing the dummies when a bunch of hoodlums rode by on their skateboards. Can you believe it? They threw bricks through the front window."

Turning to the police, Melanie asked, "Did you catch them? Where are they?"

Gloria shook her head. "By the time they got here, those guys were long gone,"

"We're checking the neighborhoods and will file the report. The detectives will check the street cameras. You can file a claim with your insurance for now." He wrote a number on his business card and handed it to Melanie. "Here's the file number."

"I already have a file number." Melanie scrolled her phone and gave it to the officer. "I have an open case."

"I'll cross-reference it to this one. Call in a few days. Maybe we'll have some information. Sorry for the mess." He looked at Gloria. "You sure I can't transport you to the ER?"

"I'm fine."

He nodded and turned to the squad car.

"Officer?" Melanie asked, "When was the last time vandalism like this happened? Around here?"

"There have been similar incidences, but mostly after hours. We couldn't identify them. They were surprisingly good at hiding from the video surveillance."

Melanie drew a breath. "Like professionals or something?"

"Or vandals who do this a lot. Call us if you need anything. We'll be doing extra patrols." The officer nodded.

Melanie yanked off her jacket and bent to pick up the broken glass. Carefully she placed the pieces in wastebaskets that the employees had brought out. A pickup truck drove up with plywood sheets in the back, and a medium-height man jumped out. He hugged Gloria and spoke in Spanish. She waved him off playfully, assuring him she was fine. Gloria introduced her husband and explained he would board up the windows for now.

"I mean, if it's okay with you. I called him right away."

"Of course, thank you."

"Yeah, no worries. I'm going inside. I'll call the insurance company." Gloria left.

Melanie nodded and continued sweeping and picking up debris. The tedious work slipped into the dinner hour, so Melanie ordered pizza delivery. The refrigerator had just been stocked with drinks, and everyone took a break.

Gloria emerged from the shop. Her lips pressed together.

"Give it to me." Melanie breathed deep, bracing for the worst. "Insurance lapsed?"

"No. We're good there, but the deductible is $5,000. I guess Nina needed a lower premium. Good thing Tito's not here. They always fought about that stuff."

It might as well be $5 million, Melanie thought. She stared at Gloria's cut brow and sighed. At least she was okay, but what next? Who next? Melanie glanced at her soiled suit and wanted to pray, but she just didn't know how.

CHAPTER 12

Melanie picked up Lacey at her parents' home and did her best to cover her emotions. Her dirty suit didn't help to dissuade them, but she made it sound like random vandalism. She kept her suspicions about who did it to herself. Confident that it was the landlord's doing, she drove home with the anxious secrets stirring inside.

As they pulled in, the neighbor stood at the bottom of the stairs. "Hey, ladies? Need an escort to your door?"

Lacey looked around. "Where did you come from?"

He shrugged. "A meeting."

Melanie looked down at her skirt, smudged with dirt. When she swiped down, she winced and stared at her hand. Red streaks stained the beige linen, and she pulled a tiny shard of glass from her hand.

"Are you okay there?" The neighbor pointed.

"Mom! You're bleeding."

"I'm fine. Let's go. I'm exhausted."

The neighbor smiled. "After you."

They all plodded up, and he stopped. "Can I get you a band-aid? Some first aid?"

At the risk of being rude, Melanie waved him off. She gulped hard, not sure she could hold it together. Once inside,

Lacey wet a towel and washed Melanie's hand. She pulled a bandage from the drawer and wrapped it around the cut finger.

A few more tears fell, and Melanie chuckled. "I'll never get this blood out." Her lips pressed tightly at first, but then a bubble of laughter escaped. "It's my favorite suit." She wiped the back of her hand across her face.

Lacey hugged her mom. "Can I get you anything?"

"No, thanks, sweetie. It's been a long day. Why don't you head to bed?" She squeezed her daughter's hand.

"If you're sure you're okay?" Lacey hugged her. "Goodnight, Mom. I love you."

The "I love you" erased her angst one notch, but when Lacey's door closed, Melanie dropped into the kitchen chair, slinking down, allowing her mind to sink as well. *What was she supposed to do?* Nothing was certain, and loneliness followed her despair.

Knock. Knock.

The sound jolted her, and she straightened.

Knock. Knock.

"Hey neighbor, it's me. From next door?" The voice was soft.

Melanie grabbed a kitchen towel and swiped at her tears. She smiled. *Oh, why not*, she thought and opened the door, pushing out the screen.

"Well, I'd say you look great, but you're a mess."

Laughing, Melanie said nothing as she wiped her cheeks and eyes again.

"Can I come in?" He raised his hand, holding a bag with a cellophane window. Chocolate chip cookies peeked out.

"Only because of those." She pointed, then waved him in. "Can I make you some decaf?" She walked into the kitchen, and he followed.

"Milk is good if you have some?"

He looked around. Melanie had never invited him in before.

"Wow! You have a lot of plants."

"Yes, I guess it's my addiction." Her eyes widened as she recalled his meetings. "Oh, I didn't mean…I just tend to overdose on living plants…." She wiped her forehead. "I…I…"

His brows furrowed. "Wait, do you think I'm an addict or something?"

"Oh no… but you said you go to meetings…." She blinked, and heat rose within her. "And that's good…." The night had gotten the best of her.

"I was at a youth meeting. Not rehab. Although sometimes I feel like those kids need rehabbing." He smiled. "I take it you had a rough day."

"Sort of." She set down a glass of milk. "Here you go… uh…." She stared.

"It's Todd." This time he laughed. "You didn't know my name, did you?"

"I'm sorry. I've been so busy."

"You think? I don't know anyone who works as much as you."

"What do you mean?" *How does he know?*

"You leave early, you come home late, and you're always wearing those suits." He reached over and picked a clump of dirty fuzz stuck to her jacket. "Well, maybe not quite like that one. And, you never have people over, either."

Melanie picked up a cookie and took a bite. "Mmm. Wow, these are fantastic."

"I take it you don't eat sweets too much?" He picked up a cookie too. "These are from the grocery store bakery. I'll have to take you to a real French bakery."

She popped the rest of the cookie in her mouth, but before chewing, she scrunched her face. *Did he say, take me?* She dusted off her fingers. "No, that's okay. I bake. I don't need to go to a bakery. I…"

"Relax. I'm not asking you on a date. But what do you do? For fun, I mean?"

Melanie felt herself flush. It had been so long since she'd spent any time alone with a man. Even on a friendly basis, she was a bit rusty.

"Well, I go to my parents a lot for dinner. Lacey and I go shopping and out to eat. We're homebodies too, and we love watching old black and white movies."

Todd sat up straight. "Casablanca? That's my favorite."

"That's everyone's favorite who doesn't watch the classics."

"Seriously?"

"Yes, seriously." Melanie narrowed her yes. "So, what's Humphrey Bogart's name in Casablanca?"

"Humphrey Bogart's in Casablanca? I thought that was James Cagney."

She laughed and grabbed another cookie. "See!" It felt good to laugh.

"I'm just kidding. Rick. His name was Rick, and hers was Elsa."

"I'm impressed."

"So, what happened?" Todd pointed to her attire.

"What didn't happen? I recently inherited a bridal shop, I'm getting kicked out, and someone vandalized the building today, and the insurance deductible is $5,000."

Leaning back, Todd pressed his shoulders into the ladder-back chair and crossed his arms. "Is that all? I thought it was something life-threatening." The front legs of his chairs set down. "But that guy at the park. I'd say that was life threatening."

She nodded and reached for another cookie but stopped.

"Oh, go ahead. You only live once." He winked. "Unless you believe in the afterlife."

Melanie pulled her hand back. *Was he a Christian?* It didn't matter. She suddenly realized that she had never tried to reach out to him. Sheepish guilt crept in.

"Do you? Believe in the afterlife?"

"Yeah. Of course."

"Do you go to church?" It wasn't her standard segue, but it might work.

"Is this an interrogation?"

"No. I was just wondering." Melanie closed her eyes and sighed.

He laughed. "Yes, I go to church. Grace Chapel, just around the corner. You?"

"Faith Community. I've attended there forever with my parents. Well, not forever, but it seems like it." She often thought of forever when her life began with Christ.

"So, you do believe in the afterlife."

"I do. Absolutely." Melanie relaxed. The tenseness in her shoulders seemed to dissipate, and her eyes no longer stung.

"Good. Then you know God's got this, right? All this," he made a circle with his finger, "will pass."

Melanie smiled. "Thanks for the reminder." She leaned forward a little, wanting badly to hug him.

"Sure." He stood. "Well, I have to work in the morning." Reaching over, he touched her shoulder. "I'll be praying for you, Melanie."

His touch reached her heart, and a coziness spread through her. She searched his face,the tousled blond hair falling over his warm brown eyes. It felt so different from the feeling she'd had for Chris way back when. This was nice, sweet—kind of pure.

"I sure appreciate it. Really, I do. You have no idea how much I needed this."

"Sure, but God did." He waved a hand towards the cookies. "Save some for Lacey."He let himself out, and Melanie watched as the door closed. She knew nothing about him, and up until tonight, she didn't have time for him. *Wow. When had life gotten in the way?* And how could she ignore anyone whom God had placed in her path? She'd been so busy with her own problems she'd forgotten to care for her neighbor, but he had not forgotten her.

After showering and dressing in soft pajamas, she crawled into bed and reached for her bible. Somehow, peace came easier tonight, and she knew she'd sleep well. If only it would last.

~

Waking refreshed, Melanie went for a quick run before getting Lacey to school. After dropping her off, she arrived at the shop before opening. She shook her head at the ugly boarded-up building, but her spirits lifted when she read the beautifully painted words on the plywood. "Come on in! Still, Open for Business," Colorful flowers embellished the corners.

Gloria sat at the front desk, a small bandage over one eye. "You're here early."

"Got my run in first thing. Listen, we need to talk."

"Sure." She swiveled in her chair.

"Tito said that Nina had no reserve for the deductible. I have some savings, but I'm more concerned about this happening again. We have to do something."

"Well, I guess we can move out. Find another building. Cheaper rent, maybe." Gloria didn't sound convinced of the latter.

"We could, but it would take time. Maybe time this guy won't give us. Or we could sell the shop?" Melanie grimaced. "That's not sounding too bad right now, is it?"

"To him? You're kidding, right?"

"Of course not to him. I'd rather liquidate our assets and close than do that. I could put it on the market right away. What else can I do? You got hurt. He threatened me, and who knows what else he'll do?"

"Don't say that!" Gloria's eyes widened, and she glanced around as if a curse were lurking.

Melanie stared at the front door. The curse just walked in.

"Hello, ladies." The landlord's lawyer stared back at the boarded-up window. He made an annoying tsk with his tongue. "What happened?"

"Why don't you tell us." Gloria glared.

Placing a hand on Gloria's arm, Melanie squeezed. "What do you want?"

"Well, we heard about your mishap yesterday, and we'd like to help."

"Mishap? Really?" Melanie crossed her arm, leaning on one hip.

"Your landlord will fix the windows immediately. The structural damage is on him, but he's also offering to help cover minimal inventory damage."

"Good, fix the windows." Gloria tilted her chin upward. "We got insurance for our inventory."

"Why would he do that?" Melanie asked.

"If you agree, you'll also be agreeing to move out in thirty days."

"We have a three…." Melanie frowned, "make that a two-month extension. Why would we agree?"

"Well, scheduling repairs can take time." He smirked. "Has the public building inspector come by?"

"Of course not. It just happened yesterday."

"Well, health ordinances stipulate that you need to get this damage repaired immediately, or they can shut you down. Not to mention the Fire Marshall. You wouldn't want your employees compromised, would you?"

"Since when do you care about our employees." Gloria hissed.

He ignored her, staring at Melanie. "Our offer expires in twenty-four hours." He didn't wait for an answer and walked to the exit.

"That's what you said a month ago!" Melanie yelled after him.

When he left, Gloria rose and faced three gawking employees. She spoke rapidly in Spanish, and the girls disbursed. Melanie headed to the back office.

"Where are you going? We have to figure this out."

"Give me a few minutes." Melanie closed the door and leaned against it. *God, what should I do? Tell me because I just don't know.*

Her shoulders slumped, and a knot stuck in her throat. Glancing at the fax machine, she noticed a small pink box resting atop it. She picked it up and slid a finger under the taped edge. It popped open, and her eyes widened at the giant, gooey, gourmet chocolate chip cookie inside. She pulled the lid down, looking for a store label. Nothing. Breaking off a piece, she savored it as the chocolate melted in her mouth and the sweet soft cookie rolled around her taste buds. Melanie smiled and thought of Todd. *This, too, will pass.* How did he know where she worked?

Melanie opened the door and looked out. "Gloria? Who brought the cookie?" She held a small chunk in her hand and mumbled, "It is so delicious!"

"Seriously? My daughter gave that to me. To cheer me up. I forgot I left it in your office."

The cookie clumped in her mouth as she tried to sludge it down. Melanie swallowed hard. "Oh my. I'm so sorry. Where'd she gets it? I'll buy you another."

"No worries, you saved me the calories."

"No, really? Where'd she get it?"

"I don't know. Some little French bakery near her house. She stopped by early this morning, but I think you need it more than me."

"You have no idea." Melanie smiled.

"Okay, ready to talk now?"

"Sure, come sit down."

The women discussed their repair options. If the landlord dragged his feet on the repairs, it could cost them time they didn't have. Melanie felt they shouldn't wait on him. Gloria phoned her husband for construction advice, and he assured her he could do the repairs for a minimal price.

"Well, why don't we do that then? Don't you think?" Said Melanie.

"Yes, but he's not charging for his labor."

"Yes, he is. I insist." Melanie had her savings, but she'd listed it in her assets for the bank loan. *No matter*, she thought. "Let's hire your husband to do the work. How soon can we get started?"

"Maybe two days. He has to order the glass. But that won't stop this guy. Melanie, he wants us out now."

"Right. He's desperate. I'm guessing he has an offer from a commercial developer for this property. I'll call a realtor and have him look for a building for us." Melanie breathed deep. Her sigh, a little too exasperated. All this was taking time away from her passion, wedding planning. Still, she couldn't leave Gloria, Tito, or her employees high and dry. She prayed everyone would be safe for now.

"Melanie, if you need to sell, go ahead. We're all fine. In a couple of months, I'll get my Social Security."

As if Gloria had read her mind, Melanie thanked God for the assurance that everything would somehow work out.

CHAPTER 13

Two days went by, and Gloria's husband was still waiting on the glass. Melanie never replied to the landlord's newest offer to pay for the repairs, but she hadn't heard from him either. She hated looking over her shoulder at every corner. Trusting was difficult.

She spent the day searching for new designs and ordered dress samples, being careful not to get sidetracked, spending the entire morning daydreaming of white lace and satin. However, that was easy today. Ordering wedding dress samples for a business that might not be here tomorrow was like a bride planning a wedding that might not be. Melanie shook at the horrible thought. She continued pouring time into posting on social media, inadvertently promoting the shop on Tiktok, Instagram, and Facebook. Closing her laptop, she leaned back and rolled her head around, cracking her neck. She heard voices. Male voices.

Stepping out of her office, Melanie smiled at a bride standing in front of a mirror. Women surrounded the bride, but no men. Melanie peered around a rack to the front of the shop. A man casually dressed in a polo shirt and slacks with a clipboard in hand stood talking with Gloria. Melanie approached.

"Here's the owner, Melanie Thompson." Gloria opened a palm towards her.

"I'm the public building inspector."

That was fast.

"I need to check the damage. Make a report on any safety issues." He clicked his pen too many times.

"I'm sorry, who sent you? We've already contracted for the repairs."

His eyes shifted back and forth. "Uh, the insurance company called."

Melanie didn't know how all this worked, but it made little sense that an insurance company would call the building inspector.

Gloria turned to Melanie. "Did you file a claim?"

"I didn't."

Gloria turned on the building inspector. "Why would they call you?"

His eyes shifted, and his pale face flushed red, all the way to his thinning hairline. "Well, maybe it was the building owner? I was just assigned the case." He opened the black clipboard notebook, and his pen glided across the page. "I have a form to fill out. Mind if I go around and look?"

"No, go right ahead. Gloria, would you mind accompanying him?"

"Not at all. My pleasure." Gloria stood and followed the man. Her elbows almost touched his as he poked around the damaged window and jotted down notes.

"And make sure you get a copy of the report," said Melanie. "And sign nothing!"

The building inspector never sent a report. Gloria's husband had installed the windows, and everything was good as new.

A few mornings later, Melanie drove to the shop when her

cell rang. Her bank registered on her car screen. Still driving, Melanie let it go to voicemail. She needed to collect her thoughts and pray. After a few minutes, she checked the voicemail.

MRS. THOMPSON, I HAVE THE STATUS OF YOUR LOAN APPLICATION. PLEASE CALL ME FOR AN APPOINTMENT TO DISCUSS IT.

Melanie's pulse quickened. The business loan was the ticket. She knew it, and she made the appointment that very afternoon. But Friday was the only day of the week when she picked up Lacey herself. It was their tradition to go out at the end of the week. *Oh, just this once, she thought.* She phoned her mother.

"Hey, Mom, how's it going?" She put the cell on speaker and laid it down.

"Your dad is stubborn." Patricia huffed.

Melanie picked up the cell. "What's up with him now?"

"Something is off. He's a little sluggish today, and I can't get him to go to the doctor."

"I'm fine!" A voice called in the background.

"You are not!" Patricia yelled. "So, did you need something, Mel?"

"Oh, no. I was going to ask if you could pick Lacey up from school, but that's okay. Better stay home with Dad." Melanie blew out a quiet breath. She'd change her appointment.

"Don't be silly. I can drag him along. Besides, maybe Lacey can help me coax him to Urgent Care."

"Never happen!" Rick yelled again.

"Don't worry about it, Melanie. We'll get her and bring her back here."

"Are you sure, mom? I sure appreciate it. I have an afternoon appointment."

"Don't give it another thought. We'll get her."

Even after hanging up, she still had a troublesome doubt. But her father hadn't had any more angina attacks, and she convinced herself that a ride might do him good. The meeting distracted her, and the thought of a shop of her own without any baggage filled her mind crowding out a nagging concern.

~

"Mrs. Thompson. I know you're eager to progress here. Please, have a seat." The Loan Officer offered a chair.

"Yes. I appreciate your seeing me this afternoon." Melanie sat on the edge of the chair.

The woman's eyes shifted downward. "Well, I'm sorry that I don't have good news. The bank denied your loan." She clasped her hands and rested them on a file. Her lips pursed.

Melanie stared and said nothing. *No. Everything is going all wrong.* Her throat dried up, and she found it hard to swallow. Her mind blanked, and she blurted, "But what if I got a co-signer?"

Her phone vibrated, startling her, but she ignored it.

"Yes, absolutely. That would make a difference. But you said you didn't...."

Melanie's phone rang. She'd forgotten to mute it. Again, she ignored it.

"Are you sure you don't need to get that?"

"No, it's fine. I'm sorry. You were saying?"

"Do you have a co-signer?" She was blunt. "At our last meeting—"

Melanie's phone vibrated again, and she huffed.

The loan officer smiled. "Why don't you get that. It could be important."

She pulled out the cell and stared. "It's from my daughter. I'm sorry, I need to check this text."

THEY'RE TAKING GRANDPA TO THE HOSPITAL. HE DOESN'T LOOK SO GOOD.

Melanie stared wide-eyed at the woman. "I'm sorry. I have to go now."

"Is everything all right?"

"No. It's my father. I have to go." Stepping out of the glass office, Melanie punched Lacey's number.

"Lacey, what's wrong with Grandpa?"

Sobs flooded the line making it difficult for Melanie to understand Lacey's words. "Lacey, please! Honey…What?… Oh, no! I'm on my way…What hospital?"

Melanie rushed out. Her cell rang again as she jumped into her car. She ignored it and drove frantically to the hospital. Parking erratically, she ran in.

"Mr. Felling, Rick Felling. He's my father." The ER nurse stood and led Melanie through the double doors to a curtained-off bed. She could hear crying, loud wailing. When she peeked around the curtain, she clutched her throat.

"Daddy!"

Her mother laid across her father's still body. No machines, no tubes. Nothing.

"What's going on?" Melanie's eyes widened.

Lacey sat curled up in a chair. Her face was buried on her knees. Her body rocked back and forth, and Melanie's cell rang again. She silenced it just before her mother cried out.

"Rick, come back to me! What will I do without you?" Patricia gripped her husband's entire lifeless body as if someone were trying to tear him away from her.

A nurse walked in, and Melanie spun around. She clutched the nurse's arm. "Please. I just got here. What happened?"

～

The small, serene chapel was empty except for mother and daughter. Candles flickered in the dim light. Melanie held Lacey tightly, and she rested her head on Lacey's. Just when they felt they had no more tears, the sobs welled up and poured out all over again.

Pastor Leland had arrived, and he stayed with Patricia in the ER. A social worker RN joined them, waiting for the body handlers to come to take Rick's body to the mortuary. Melanie shivered, even thinking about it. But Lacey couldn't be present, so the nurse promised to send someone to the chapel to retrieve the girls after it happened. Melanie's cell rang again.

"Who keeps calling?" She ignored it.

"It's Aunt Charlene. I called her earlier." Lacey's first words.

Melanie picked up her cell and pressed her sister's number. Before Charlene answered, a text came through.

IT'S YOUR MOTHER. PLEASE COME TO THE ER.

CHAPTER 14

The girls ran down the hospital corridors. Nurses and visitors gave reprimanding glances as they swept by. Gaining admittance, they burst through the doors and rushed to the curtained-off bay where Rick was. Two men commenced wheeling out a covered body. She was sure it was her father. They had covered him from head to toe with a sheet. Melanie spun around and grabbed Lacey. *But where was her mom?* She pulled Lacey to her chest and shaded her eyes from the scene behind. Melanie tensed every muscle to keep her body from shaking.

A nurse jogged towards them. "Miss? Excuse me. You went the wrong way. Your mother is down this hallway. Come, I'll take you."

Patricia sat with a tissue pressed to her face. Her eyes were red, and her face flushed. Her blood pressure had risen so high that blood ran from her nose and spurted from her tear ducts. Red-stained tissue and gauze pads lay everywhere.

Pastor Leland ushered the girls in and uttered something about making room as he left. He stepped out of the busy cubicle.

Another residing physician asked, "I'm assuming you're a relative?" He didn't wait for an answer. "We cauterized the inside of her nostrils to control the bleeding. In just a matter of seconds, it should stop. We're giving her medication to lower her blood pressure. She gave us some of her medical history."

Melanie fought to hold back tears. "She's my mother. I know she has hypertension, and she takes medication...."

"Yes, she told us that." He looked at Patricia and patted her arm. "You've all had quite a shock today already. Let's give her some time to recoup." Kind eyes replaced the stoic bedside manner earlier. "I'm so sorry for your loss. Let's give her a few minutes now, but I think she should stay overnight."

Lacey sobbed and rushed to her grandmother.

A kind nurse took her by the shoulders. "Is there anyone else here? Your dad, another relative? Someone who can sit with you in the waiting area. I'm sorry, we need to keep your grandmother calm."

Lacey glanced at her grandmother, then stared at her mom, her frightened face streaked. She gulped. "I'm okay. I want to stay." Taking gasping breaths, she rubbed her face with her sleeve. "My Grandma, will she be okay?"

"Yes, she will. I know it's frightening. You've all had quite a jolt, and I'm so sorry, but we'll get her managed. I promise." The nurse patted Lacey and moved her to a chair on the far side of the room. She smiled and whispered. "I'll be praying for her."

Melanie nodded. The words filled the reservoir behind her eyes, but they gave strength to her heart.

"Mom? How are you feeling? What's going on?"

Patricia sat on the bed, an IV in her arm, and gauze up her nostrils. Her eyes were red and swollen. "They took him, Melanie. He's gone." She sobbed. "I can't live without him."

Melanie squeezed her mother's shaking, fragile body. "I know, Mom. I know."

They heard a knock on the wall, and a curtain pulled

aside. Pastor Leland peeked and stepped to Patricia's bedside. He looked at Lacey, sitting in the corner.

"Come here, kiddo."

She joined them, and he enveloped them all as best he could. Tears splashed from his face as he prayed, and his soothing words bathed their battered souls. Quiet sobs flowed, and God settled the peace upon them that surpasses all understanding.

Charlene flew into town overnight, and she and Melanie spoke little. They moved as if in a dream. A surreal experience for sure. A horrible nightmare. Patricia stayed in the hospital, and Lacey slept in the room with her, never leaving her side. They released her the next day, and they all returned to Patricia and Rick's house. Empty loneliness and painful sorrow filled the once cheerful home.

A few days of stoic silence passed, and finally, Melanie forced herself to think about something other than losing her dad. She thought about the business, and after a morning of contemplation and prayer, she called her lawyer. Mr. Randall gave wise counsel, and Melanie knew urgent decisions were in order. Thirty minutes later, she hung up.

Charlene sat at the kitchen table, sipping coffee, and Melanie walked in. She gazed at her father's chair and willed herself to imagine him there. His presence was everywhere, so it wasn't hard. But his voice was silenced—his loving encouragement, wisdom, and sometimespushy advice were gone, forever. The ache burned in her heart and permeated every inch of her body. It hurt so much to face the reality of him not being here. Here with them, ever again.

"So, I never heard exactly what happened. I know the ambulance took him to the ER." Charlene gripped her mug.

Melanie rubbed her forehead and closed her eyes. "I asked

Mom to pick Lacey up at school. I had an appointment with the bank. Dad insisted on driving instead, and when Lacey got to the car, he was slumped and unresponsive. Mom was hysterical, so Lacey called 911 and me."

"She phoned me, too. She's a strong girl, Melanie." Charlene's lip curved upwards. "Like us."

"I left my appointment right away, but by the time I got there, he was gone."

Melanie didn't think she had tears left, but one by one, they slid from the corner of her eyes. Her mother's words haunted her. Yes, what would she do without him? Melanie knew what Daddy would say, trust God. But his faith was more substantial than hers, and she relied on his strength, his direction, his guidance. At this moment, she doubted if she could do anything without him. *How could life go on?* If only she'd listened to him. He never wanted the bank loan, and that's where she was when he died.

"I should have waited. Daddy never wanted me to take out a business loan. And I could have made the appointment for the following week. Then I still could have picked up Lacey myself in the afternoon."

"Stop it, Mel. This wasn't your fault."

Her eyes burned. "But I just couldn't wait. I rushed ahead on my own."

"On your own is not a bad thing."

"But Dad. He's always right."

"No, Mel. He's not. No one is."

"I should have listened to him, but I didn't, and now, it was all for nothing. I thought for sure the bank loan was the answer to all my problems."

"Wait, it wasn't?" Charlene sat up straight.

Her question stopped the tears, and Melanie welcomed the guilt it brought. "Didn't I tell you? I didn't get the loan. No collateral."

Charlene pushed her mug away. "Are you kidding me? Why didn't you call me?"

"Not now, sis." She took a tissue. "We have work to do."

Surprised that Charlene didn't challenge her, they began the arduous task of making funeral arrangements for their father. Their mother slept, and by late morning, Charlene glanced at the wall clock and stood.

"It's almost noon. I need a break." Charlene walked outside and returned with the mail. She sifted through the stack and dropped one letter on the table.

Melanie glanced at it. A plain ecru-colored envelope was addressed to Mr. Rick Felling. It looked like a personal letter. With so much electronic communication, private mail was a rarity. Intrigued, Melanie stared. There was no return address in the corner. She reached for the letter opener.

Charlene took it from Melanie's hands. "What are you doing? That's not yours."

"Really? And how is Daddy going to open it?"

"Leave it, sis. We don't have to handle everything today. Not now. It can wait. We haven't even had the memorial yet." Charlene walked into the kitchen.

She wasn't one to intentionally inflict guilt, but Melanie felt it coming in all directions and took Charlene's words as cruel, but felt she deserved it. A tear splashed, staining the smooth linen envelope.

In the kitchen, casseroles and desserts from the church covered the counters. Melanie watched as Charlene lifted a foil-wrapped dish, picking at the homemade macaroni and cheese inside. The house was perfumed with flowers, and a basket filled with condolences cards overflowed on the coffee table. But none of it comforted Melanie. She just wanted her father.

Charlene walked over and pressed a hand on her shoulder. They sat in silence until a shrill scream came from the bedroom.

"Grandma!"

The sisters ran, bursting into the master bedroom. Lacey sat on her knees on Patricia's bed, gently shaking her grandmother.

"Grandma! Grandma!" Lacey reached for Melanie. "She said her head hurt, then her neck went stiff, and she went all quiet. Mom, help her, please!"

Charlene was already on her phone. "I'm calling 911."

Melanie grabbed her mother's hands and prayed. She begged, and she pleaded. She glanced at Lacey, and the sight of her fifteen-year-old daughter, experiencing grief as no one should, gave rise to anger. She wanted to shout at God. *How can you do this to us?* But a supernatural strength gave her the wisdom to call Pastor Leland instead. The paramedics came. *Not again, not again, God, please.*

Pastor Leland waited for them in the ER. He hugged Lacey and the receptionist asked them to wait. The déjà vu was too much. Melanie stepped outside. It was raining now. Not a hopeful sign. All dark and no light. The steady drizzle dampened the ground enough to raise a steamy, oily asphalt smell. Melanie covered her nose and walked inside.

A nurse ushered Melanie, Lacey, and Pastor Leland back to an empty hallway. The nurse's body language held no urgency, but Lacey rushed ahead. Charlene was waiting, and her jaw so tense, the veins bulged in her neck. Her arms wrapped tightly around her body. A doctor stood close by.

"Charlene?" Melanie's eyes pleaded with her sister.

"I'm so sorry." A young doctor stared back. "Your mother suffered a massive brain hemorrhage."

Lacey spun around. "What does that mean?" She looked at each person. Her eyes pleading.

The doctor stared at the sisters, who remained silent. Then he nodded at Pastor Leland. Melanie caught the exchange, and her brow furrowed. She just wanted to hear that her mother would recover. She had to.

"She's in a coma. We don't expect her to make it through the night. I'm sorry. There is nothing we can—"

Charlene raised a hand. "We get it. Thanks."

Melanie grabbed Lacey. A painful wail rang throughout the ER...again.

"Take your time. I'm so sorry." The doctor slipped out.

Once again, Pastor Leland recited scripture. He read Psalms 33. At first, his tone strained, but as he read, it was as if the scriptures gave strength and his voice resonated strong comfort.

CHAPTER 15

Pastor Leland and the church took over all the arrangements for the double funeral. The girls alternated on who would not be attending. At any given moment, one or the other expressed that they just couldn't handle the double funeral. But a week later, when the day arrived, they all attended. As expected, the memorial and burial overwhelmed them all, and the traditional "Let's all meet at the house afterward" didn't happen. Instead, the church held a reception in the Community Hall, and Pastor Leland urged the girls to do what was best for themselves. They asked him to express their thanks and quietly left.

The girls plopped on separate couches and chairs at the house. Lacey curled up in her grandfather's favorite recliner, and Melanie sat at the kitchen counter, her mother's clean glass tea mug resting in its place. Charlene then walked out back into the garden and began weeding.

The doorbell rang, but Lacey didn't stir, and Melanie contemplated ignoring it but opened the door instead. Tito and his family greeted her. In front stood, who Melanie guessed, was Tito's son. A spark of light shined in her dark life.

Last week, after her mother's death, Melanie decided to get rid of the shop. She was sure that she didn't want it anymore. Mr. Randall followed her instructions and gifted her inheritance to Gloria and Tito. If they didn't want the headache, the alternative was to shut it down, give everyone a decent severance package, as funds allowed, and sell the business as quickly as possible. Her primary concern was to prevent any further injury to anyone. Melanie couldn't even think about the threat of continuing danger that the landlord imposed. Tito and Gloria had accepted the offer.

Melanie smiled at the teenager and knew she had made the right decision.

He grinned so widely that his eyes almost shut. His short arms hung by his side, thumbs turned inward. A striped t-shirt tucked into new blue jeans hugged his round protruding stomach. Melanie never knew Tito had a special needs child.

"We went to the service but weren't able to reach you before you left. Gloria, too." Tito looked down.

"I'm sorry we didn't stay long."

"Please, don't apologize. This is my wife, Maria, and my son, Tito."

The boy's father nudged his son forward. He held out a bouquet of white hydrangeas and greens as he lifted it towards her. It covered his entire face, but he peeked out, grinning broadly. Melanie couldn't help but smile. She took the flowers. "It's nice to meet you, Tito and Maria."

Maria swiped a tear and nodded.

Tito cleared his throat. "We're so sorry, Melanie." His voice cracked.

Melanie could only nod and reached out and patted the son. Though her grief was unbearable, meeting their son put things into perspective. Tito and his wife didn't have it easy themselves, and it was visibly apparent. Melanie wondered that Tito had never said a word.

The son wrapped his plump arms around Melanie's waist and squeezed. His mother reached to pull him back, but Melanie hugged him tightly.

"We also want to thank you for the shop. But if you change your mind…."

"No, I won't. But that's very thoughtful of you."

"Melanie, we want you with us. We can work out the finances. God will work it out." Tito made the sign of the cross.

It warmed Melanie's heart, and she took it as confirmation that she had done the right thing. The boy still gripped Melanie, and she spoke over him. "Thank you, Tito. Thank you so much. But I never wanted the shop. It's yours and Gloria's. Do whatever you'd like with it." She looked into the boy's eyes. "And take good care of this guy."

They nodded, and the entire family hugged Melanie before parting.

The days lingered as Charlene and Melanie went through papers, met with the lawyer, and made some decisions. Melanie was able to break the lease on her apartment, and as they were moving, the neighbor, Todd, helped with some last items. He stood with his hands on his hips.

"Sorry to see you go. I'd ask for your phone number, but maybe you need some time?"

She didn't answer.

"Or maybe I'm a little too late in asking."

Melanie wished she'd felt something, but she didn't. "I don't know where I'll land up. But I sure appreciate your help."

"What help?" He waved around. "You pretty much got it covered."

Lacey stepped out, lugging a box.

Todd ruffled her hair. "Hey, kiddo, can I get that for you?"

She set it down and went back in without saying a word.

"If there's anything you need. I'd be happy to help."

"Well, the cookies and the talk were perfect timing." Melanie just wished that were all it took to ease her pain this time.

Todd drew a hand through his sun-bleached hair. "Yeah, well, that was a God thing. I should have listened to Him and come over sooner."

"Last one, mom." Lacey brought out another box.

"Hey, can I pray with you guys?" He touched both their shoulders.

With eyes wide open, Lacey gaped. "You're a Christian?"

"Ouch," he said. "I guess not an obvious one. I'll work on it." He winked at Lacey.

Breathing deep, Melanie thought. *I will too.*

CHAPTER 16

The plan was to move into her parent's house until they sold it. As painful as that would be, it was only temporary. Melanie couldn't pay the mortgage on her income, and the hospital, ambulance, and paramedic bills for both Rick and Patricia were piling up. Even with medical insurance and life insurance policies, she doubted there would be any reserve for Charlene or herself.

Charlene had flown back into town to help them move into her parents' house for the time being. They had a lot to do to get the house ready for sale, but Charlene pushed the girls to move to D.C. anyway. Charlene insisted it was the best option for them, but Melanie wondered if her sister needed it too. It sounded promising, but she didn't want Charlene to support her and Lacey, and that's what would happen, at least for a while.

"I don't think so, Charlene. My business is here."

"What business? You gave away the shop. You wouldn't let me co-sign for the bank loan."

"But I can still work from home."

"What home? You have no home." Charlene's voice rose.

"I'll get another apartment. I've supported Lacey and me

just fine." Melanie shrugged. "Who cares about a building? I don't need the headache, anyway."

"Melanie, come on. You know you wanted your own office."

She did, but was it just to prove something? Had she been trying to appease the heartache she'd caused her dad? She knew he was proud of her. He said so. But would she forever be trying to make things better? If only they were still here.

"Maybe, someday. I guess it's just not God's plan right now."

Charlene glared. "God's plan? How can you even believe He has one after all this?"

Melanie bit her lip. She wouldn't go there with her sister. Not now. Charlene's anger had not subsided, and it was all directed at God. "I know He does, Charlene. And He has one for you, too. Let's just leave it at that."

Both sat at the dining table once again, and Charlene sifted through the stack of mail.

Looking at her watch, Melanie stood and hugged her sister. "I'll be late for my appointment with a bride. Say a prayer for me." But she knew Charlene wasn't open to prayer right now.

"I guess you need it. You don't have the booking yet."

"Thanks for the vote of confidence, sis."

Charlene picked up a stack of mail. Flipping through the envelopes, she stopped and pulled one out. "Wait, you never opened this letter." She fingered an embossed seal on the back of the ecru envelope, and her eyes widened. "Hey, it's from a Restoration Grant Foundation in Bay Town, Mississippi."

"What?" Melanie took the envelope and tapped it against her hand. "Charlene, the appointment I have is with a bride from Mississippi. Well, New Orleans, but originally from Mississippi."

"Really?" Charlene's eyes widened. "Is she from Bay Town?"

"I don't know." Melanie shrugged. "If she is, will you believe that maybe there's a divine plan at work here?"

"Yeah. I don't think so. But if that's a yes, there...I might be a believer."

Melanie opened the envelope.

Her fingers tingled, and she felt hopeful with the letter in hand and the appointment with Summer. Ripping open the envelope, she heard her father's voice. *It's a long shot.* She breathed deep and stopped for a moment. Her shoulders slumped, but then she remembered Pastor Leland's words from the memorial service. *Hope shines in the darkness.*

Melanie pulled out a single sheet, and her eyes glided down the page.

"Well? Did he get it?" Charlene sounded like she was about to burst.

Melanie's eyes felt heavy, and her smile faded. She dropped the paper and exhaled.

"Oh, no. Are you kidding me?" Charlene grabbed the paper and read. "Denied? Denied because you're too far away. What? Do they think you're a flight risk or something? Come on!"

Melanie walked to the door. "I'll be back this evening."

That was it. Even this appointment with Summer wouldn't change anything. Flying back and forth to Mississippi for a week or even days wasn't something she could budget right now. *What had she been thinking?* Besides, Lacey needed her too, and without her dad or mom, she just didn't have the strength to pursue it. She had to meet Summer, and she had to turn her down.

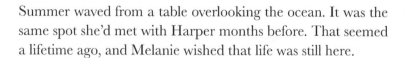

Summer waved from a table overlooking the ocean. It was the same spot she'd met with Harper months before. That seemed a lifetime ago, and Melanie wished that life was still here.

She breathed deep. Her world was so drastically now altered. How could that be in so short a time? She was thankful she had emailed Summer about her parents. Melanie didn't trust herself to break the news in person. It was too fresh.

"Hi, Summer. So good to see you. You're looking lovely, as always." Melanie twitched inside, thinking she sounded like a script.

Summer's bright smile faded as she looked back at Melanie. "I am so sorry for your loss."

"Thank you. I appreciate it." She bit her lip and opened her eyes wide, trying desperately to hold back waterworks. "Congratulations. Your fiancé finally came to his senses. Setting a date is huge."

"Yes. Is fourteen months enough time to plan the wedding of my dreams? I booked the venue with the only fall date available next year."

"Well, that's a tight time frame for a big wedding." Melanie's lips drew a straight line. Usually, she would be nothing but optimistic. "But, about that, I may not be the one to help you right now. It might be better for you to work with a local planner." Melanie's heart dropped.

For the first time since her parents passed, she thought seriously about her business. She loved doing weddings, especially ones like this, but there it went, the last hope, and it was Melanie's decision. Daddy wasn't here to help, and she felt like she couldn't take the risk. What if she failed? What if she flopped on Summer's dream? It wouldn't just be Summer's ruin. It would be hers as well. She'd lost so much already. Melanie swallowed hard.

Summer's soft face hinted at sorrow but lifted with hope. "But I trust you to do a wonderful job. Even from here."

"Thank you, but with my parents gone…well, with taking care of their estate and all."

"Is it financial? I'm sorry to be so blunt, but may I give you an advance? Whatever you need."

"You haven't even hired me yet."

"Oh, this is just formalities. I'm hiring you. I've seen nothing so spectacular as what you pulled off for Harper in Malibu."

"I'm not sure how soon I can get started. My business is on hold right now."

Summer's friendly eyes said, "I'm listening." Her heartfelt demeanor caused Melanie to spill all the obstacles to growing her business. She even shared about the grant and her dad's desire to retire in Bay Town. It was the first time she expressed it that way. Her father's passion...

His. He wanted it. Her pulse quickened. The move to Mississippi. To Bay Town. Melanie had been so preoccupied with doing the right thing to become independent, to prove herself, that she couldn't see the longing of her father's heart. She was blinded. It was his dream. That's why he had pushed so hard. He wasn't just bossy or controlling. The grant would have achieved both their dreams.

In reaching for her future, she struggled with independent decisions that she hoped would make him proud of her. It was like false humility. He was already pleased. He said that. She didn't need to earn his forgiveness from her past or prove her worthiness. Like Jesus, her father's forgiveness was a done deal. She had nothing to prove to him, and finally, she realized, but it was too late. Or was it? Guilt and humility were two different things. Then it hit her. God's grace humbled her. His grace showered her with her father's love, acceptance, and forgiveness.

"Did you say Bay Town Restoration Grant?" Summer's brows furrowed.

Melanie's mind flooded back to when she was a young girl. The fun times in the gulf. She could almost hear the gulls squawking and her nose scrunched at the sometimes stinky gulf waters. Every Friday night, her father would drive the family to Land's End for banana splits, and on Sundays, they'd eat at The Manière's Sister Restaurant. She chuckled just thinking about the crab traps on the piers and swimming in the warm gulf waters and leisurely strolls down Main Street. Those were slower, more relaxed times. No wonder he wanted to go back!

"Melanie?"

"What?" She blinked as if returning to the present. "Excuse me?"

"What was the name of the grant?" Summer raised her brows.

"The Bay Town Restoration Grant. Have you heard of it?"

Summer laughed. "I should say so. I grew up in Bay Town, but I recently moved to New Orleans. The entire family has, except for my Grandaddy. He loves Bay Town, and after the big hurricane, he formed this foundation." Summer smiled. "A restoration foundation."

Melanie couldn't speak. Her eyes widened, and her mouth gaped.

"Why Melanie, my grandaddy was probably the one who signed that letter that denied you. Shame on him!" A sultry laugh escaped. "He's such a southerner through and through and you being a Yankee and all." Summer laughed but stopped abruptly. "Hang on." She pulled out her phone, and a polished nail tapped a number.

"What are you doing?" Melanie whispered.

"Hey, Granddaddy? This is Summer…I'm fine…I'm in California…I know…I know…" Summer pulled the phone away and mouthed to Melanie. "He hates California."

Melanie chuckled. *That's probably why I didn't get the grant.* It somehow made her feel better—poor Dad. They never stood a chance.

"What, Granddaddy?… Yes, yes. I'm having lunch with

one of your prospective grant applicants...Melanie Thompson, from California....Oh, really."

"He remembers you." Summer winked. "Grandaddy, you haven't actually chosen a recipient yet, have you? ... I didn't think so. Your committee moves slower than molasses. Well, can you do me a favor and reconsider Miz Melanie Thompson? I can vouch for her... Oh, I know. The committee can squawk all they want, but we both know it's up to you... Well, you don't say. Although I am not surprised." Summer pulled the phone away. "He says your application was impressive." ... "Yes, Grandaddy. Maybe it's providential? Anyway, Miz Melanie is my good friend. In fact, she's coordinating my wedding, and she would be an exceptional asset to Bay Town...uh, huh...yes...of course...don't you think too long now. Thank you, Granddaddy. I'll see you for supper on Sunday."

Summer gently placed her phone down. She patted her lips with the white linen napkin and smiled. "Well, Miz Melanie, pack your bags, and get ready for life on the gulf!"

CHAPTER 17

M onths passed, and all the loose strings in her life were fitly tied. She should have been excited, filled with hope. But, instead of strength and trust fueling her actions, skepticism took root. Was she doing the right thing? Fear replaced faith, and she felt as if nothing could hold her broken heart together. Flooded with continuing grief, Melanie gave in to rising doubt.

Leaving California and starting a new life seemed like a good idea at first. But the west coast was all Lacey knew. Still, a fresh start. That's what Daddy said, but she needed his presence. Maybe she'd find it again in Mississippi? Some of her happiest times were in the gulf, with him, her mom, and Charlene. But that was then. Perhaps she could build new memories with Lacey. Melanie's emotions glided like a roller coaster, and she gripped onto her bible as one would hang on to dear life. Eventually, she began to hope again.

Lacey had grown a little sullen, somewhat introspective. It was to be expected, but in some ways, she seemed to have grown stronger and older in the few months following her grandparents' death. Melanie's heart ached for her daughter, but she was thankful that Lacey hadn't totally withdrawn like most teens might. Pastor Leland's counseling helped, but she did have her moments, and when sorrowful melancholy crept back into Lacey's playful nature, Melanie's heart ached even more.

Finally, Lacey seemed to welcome the move to Bay Town, and she was eager to see what Grandpa loved so much about the south. And Melanie resolved that a move would be a good change for them both.

The bridal shop was panning out to be a good thing for Tito and Gloria. They were a great team and found another building. It wasn't worth fighting to stay in Nina's old building. Melanie had a pleasant feeling and was confident in letting the business go. With all the turmoil surrounding the shop, the Lord had used it to direct Melanie to the current plan.

Charlene had made many more trips to California over the months to help with the estate and still nagged at Melanie to move to D.C. Melanie wouldn't budge. When Rick and Patricia's house sold, it surprised her that she had enough for a down payment on a small home in Bay Town after all the bills were paid. This was for real.

Summer had negotiated a fantastic deal with her grandfather for a small cottage he owned right on the gulf. He held many properties, and most were vacant, and he wouldn't rent, so selling off the little place to Melanie made him feel philanthropic.

She could never have afforded a home on the water, but he was generous in his selling price. Summer had much to do with it, of that Melanie was sure. Summer had also procured a lease on a building for Melanie's business on Main Street. This was it. It was happening. Melanie knew it wasn't just her father or Summer. It was God. She could trust Him, but deep inside, she always knew that. The trust was secure.

∾

Melanie and Lacey stood on the curb of the little suburban airport. A welcome reprieve from the hustle and bustle of Los Angeles International. This single stucco building and the outdoor terminal were reminiscent of the airports in old black and white movies.

"I feel like I'm at the airport with Rick and Elsa from Casablanca." Lacey looked around.

Melanie chuckled, but her nose perked at the smell of fresh baked goods floating out from the terminal food court. She turned, half expecting to see Todd with chocolate chip cookies. Remembering how God had brought him into her life at just the right moment, she said a prayer of thanks and let the memory of him fade. *God has other plans.* She hoped.

"Kind of iconic, isn't it?" Pastor Leland smiled.

"You can say that again." Melanie nodded at murals of 50s movie stars posing in front of old planes.

"You sure I can't take this in for you?" Pastor Leland loaded the last of the luggage onto a cart.

"No, thanks. You'll get a ticket if you leave your car. Thank you so much for everything." Her eyes burned once more. "We would have never gotten through all this without you."

He nodded. "With God, you would have. He uses many of us to ease each other's burdens. I miss your mom and dad too, Melanie. We all do. I have no answers, but you continue to trust Him. Never forget how much he loves you."

"Move along, please." A tall police officer stared as he walked by, waving his arms forward. "Loading and unloading only."

"Let me pray for you two real quick." Pastor Leland nodded at the officer.

The uniformed man passed. "Take your time, sir." He tipped his hat.

Pastor Leland's prayer immediately settled a calm over the

huddled group. He asked for God's blessing, protection, and peace. He also choked up on the Amen.

The girls dabbed their eyes, and so did he.

"Now, ladies, listen carefully. This is the best I've got. Find a good church home right away. Don't let a week go by that you don't visit a church. Keep praying. God will show you where your home will be. I wish I knew someone down there, but I'm California born and bred." His board shorts, surf tee, and flip-flops attested to that. His head-to-toe tan and longish, greying hair did as well.

Melanie nodded. "We will, Pastor. I'm sure we won't have too much trouble. It is the bible belt."

"I'll check around, too." He hugged them both. "The Lord bless and keep you, girls. I'll be praying."

When they boarded the plane, it was already full. Upon take-off, Melanie leaned over Lacey as they watched their life in California slip away. Pools and palm trees grew smaller and smaller, then finally disappeared below the clouds. Melanie tried to read. She tried to sleep, but her mind could not rest. She patted her daughter's arm as Lacey stared out the window, wetness dripping down her cheeks. Melanie hugged her.

Hours later, they made it through the flight, the layover, and finally landed in Mississippi.

"Hey, ya'll!" The beautiful tall, slender blonde waved a toned, long arm high in the air. "It is so good to see you! I can't wait to take you to the cottage." Summer bent over, hugging both Melanie and Lacey.

Melanie had never experienced this much affection from any bride-to-be before the wedding. It was a welcome distraction. Summer directed a man in a dark suit to collect all the luggage, then she hooked arms with both girls, whisking them to a large black sedan. They slipped in the back seat.

After they crossed over Lake Ponchartrain, Summer asked her driver to take the scenic route. The warm wind blew as they breezed past the serene Gulf of Mexico. They drove along the unfamiliar terrain for quite some time, and it looked nothing like a California coastline.

Lacey turned and finally spoke. "Where are the palm trees? Don't all beaches have palm trees?"

Summer smiled. "We have our charm, dear. Besides, this is the gulf, and it's a bit different than the ocean."

Melanie patted her daughter and stared out as well.

Finally, Summer sang, "And here we are, ladies!" She leaned towards the driver. "Oh, Charles, could you drive down Main Street before heading to the cottage?"

The driver turned down a quintessential downtown street complete with antique-looking lamp lights.

Summer turned to Melanie. "I do believe all your things arrived yesterday and are in the house. But I wanted you to look at the shop first."

Lacey huffed quietly. "I just want to go to the house." She whispered, "Please, Mom."

Melanie patted her daughter. "We will, sweetie." She turned and nodded at Summer. "Sure, just a quick drive-by would be nice. We're awfully tired."

Uncharacteristically, Lacey let explode her exasperation and thrust her head against the back seat. It was all catching up, and Melanie felt Lacey's pain. The mixed emotions of grieving their loss, leaving California, and just the unknown.

What in the world had she been thinking? Melanie's eyes began to burn.

"It'll be okay. We'll be all right, Lace." Melanie placed an arm around her and squeezed, trying to reassure herself as much as Lacey.

"Oh, I apologize. Where are my manners? You must be exhausted. We'll just go on to your new home." Summer gushed.

"No, please, go on by the...wait...stop!" Melanie tapped the slow driving chauffer.

A narrow two-story brick building painted white stood out against the other buildings. Mashed between an eclectic mix of vintage, retro, and trendy shops, it somehow blended. But it didn't. Illuminated by the sun's rays bouncing off the bay window, the structure glistened. Thick white molding ran along the top of the first floor, and above it, there was more brick than two framed windows with flower boxes on the sills. White wainscoting framed the front antique glass door. Etched on the glass in gold lettering was her name. 'Melanie Thompson, Wedding Planner.' The small shop boasted a bay window and scrolled across it, "Quaint Affairs." Little flourishes of gold flowers and leaves graced the corners. It was the name Melanie had chosen for her shop. Her father wasn't particularly fond of the name, but apparently, he had written it in the grant application.

Lacey sat up. "Mom? Is it yours? The shop?"

Melanie looked at Summer.

"It's hers all right. I got Grandaddy so excited that he ordered the signage himself."

Melanie breathed deep. "It's ours, Lacey."

Summer tapped the driver. "Will you please pull in front here for a moment?"

When the car parked, Lacey stepped out first and stretched. Melanie followed. She walked to the front door and ran a finger over her name. She peeked through the bay window into the empty building, imagining where her furniture would go. Perhaps she'd get those antique pieces she'd always wanted. For the first time in months, she dared to dream again.

"Anything interesting in there?" A deep friendly voice spoke behind her.

Melanie turned and stared. For the first time since her parents' death, fear and anxiety flew from her. She felt a smile breaking across her face as a friendly one smiled back at her.

Wavy dark hair fell across his forehead, and dark stubble

dotted his cheeks and chiseled jawline. A man stood casually with one hand in his jeans pocket and the other gripping a small white bag.

"In there? Anything interesting?" He repeated.

"Oh. Not yet, but soon, I hope." Melanie shrugged.

He raised his brow, and his long lashes blinked. "Are you the new owner of…" He squinted. "Quaint Affairs."

She chuckled, hearing the name of her new shop for the first time. "Yes, I am." Extending her hand, she said, "Hi, I'm Melanie Thompson."

He squeezed her hand tightly. "Nice to meet you, Melanie Thompson. I'm Desmond Brooks. Welcome to the neighborhood." He held out the bag. "Chocolate Chip Cookie?"

Before Melanie could respond, a voice yelled.

"Pastor! Hey Pastor, come on on over here and help me with this, will ya?" A woman two doors down waved, and when her eyes connected with Melanie, she yelled, "Hey, there!" Her long grayish-red hair swirled in the breeze.

Melanie waved back and stared at the eclectic shop as the woman dragged some furniture to the storefront.

Desmond Brooks breathed deep. "I better go help." He stared but didn't immediately move, but then shoved the bag of cookies in Melanie's hands. "Here, a housewarming gift."

"Pastor! Come on. This is heavy."

"Coming!" He waved and nodded back at Melanie as he left her standing there.

Lacey called, "Pastor?" Lacey squinted, staring down the street. "You found a church already?"

Melanie laughed at the banter and juggling unfolding at the vintage thrift shop a couple of doors down.

Lacey walked over, looked at the bag, and took a cookie. As she chewed, Melanie warmed inside, thankful that Lacey's appetite had returned. At least for the time being. They had a long road ahead of them still.

"I like this place, Mom." Lacey wrapped her arms around Melanie's waist.

Melanie hugged her daughter and kissed the top of her head. They stared down the sidewalk, and then Melanie glanced at the building. The old white brick building stood proud and protective.

"Thank you, Daddy, and thank you, Jesus."

The End

ACKNOWLEDGMENT AND SPECIAL THANKS:

To Valerie Bishop for her speedy reading and editing skills, to Celebrate Lit Publishing and Chautona Havig for all their help and encouragement. To Serious Scribblers, Foothill Library Writers Critique Group, and all my lovely family and friends for their support. Most of all, and always to my husband, Bruce, for his enthusiasm in this writing journey. To God be all glory. 2 Corinthians 3:18

ABOUT THE AUTHOR

Kathleen J. Robison is an Okinawan-American. Born in Okinawa, raised in California, Florida, Mississippi, and Singapore. Her travels are the inspirational settings for her stories. She and her Pastor husband have eight adult children. Seven are married, blessing them with fourteen grandchildren and counting. The diversity of their 31 family members provide the inspiration for more lively characters than can be imagined. Her husband grew up in the streets of Los Angeles raised by a single working mom, and that life provides fodder for many of the conflicts of her characters.

Tackling difficult life's trials with God's strength are the central theme of Kathleen's stories. She hopes to inspire her readers to trust God and with His strength, weather through and rise above trials and tragedies. If you like suspenseful stories with a thread of romance, you will enjoy Kathleen's Bay Town Series!

facebook.com/kathleenjrobisonauthor

instagram.com/kathleenjrobison

bookbub.com/profile/3794692396

ALSO BY KATHLEEN J. ROBISON

Bay Town Series

Shattered Guilt (Book One)

Celebrate Lit Publishing
Is proud to endorse

Roseanna White
DESIGNS

Finding the pictures to capture your words

http://www.roseannawhitedesigns.com/